"You're not going to ta

"I told Kane that i get you home safely. That's exactly what I intend to do."

"I don't need a protector, Jonas." She smiled, trying to lighten the mood, but his eyes flashed and a muscle in his jaw clenched.

"There's something you need to understand. I always finish what I start." He turned on his heel, walked to the door and opened it, disappearing inside before she could respond.

That was probably for the best.

There was nothing she could add to the conversation that would change anything. Jonas had his mission. She had hers. For now, they converged. Soon enough, they'd both fulfill their goals. When they did, they'd part ways and go on with their lives.

That was the way it was supposed to be.

That was the way she should want it to be.

She just wasn't sure she did.

Books by Shirlee McCoy

Love Inspired Suspense

Die Before Nightfall
Even in the Darkness
When Silence Falls
Little Girl Lost
Valley of Shadows
Stranger in the Shadows
Missing Persons
Lakeview Protector
*The Guardian's Mission
*The Protector's Promise
Cold Case Murder
*The Defender's Duty
**Running for Cover
Deadly Vows
**Running Scared
**Running Blind
Out of Time
**Lone Defender

*The Sinclair Brothers
**Heroes for Hire

Steeple Hill Trade

Still Waters

SHIRLEE McCOY

has always loved making up stories. As a child, she daydreamed elaborate tales in which she was the heroine—gutsy, strong and invincible. Though she soon grew out of her superhero fantasies, her love for storytelling never diminished. She knew early that she wanted to write inspirational fiction, and she began writing her first novel when she was a teenager. Still, it wasn't until her third son was born that she truly began pursuing her dream of being published. Three years later she sold her first book. Now a busy mother of five, Shirlee is a homeschool mom by day and an inspirational author by night. She and her husband and children live in Washington and share their house with a dog, two cats and a bird. You can visit her website at www.shirleemccoy.com, or email her at shirlee@shirleemccoy.com.

LONE DEFENDER

Shirlee McCoy

Love Inspired

Recycling programs for this product may not exist in your area.

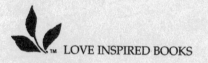 ™ LOVE INSPIRED BOOKS

ISBN-13: 978-0-373-44456-4

LONE DEFENDER

Copyright © 2011 by Shirlee McCoy

www.LoveInspiredBooks.com

Printed in U.S.A.

For you, LORD, have delivered me from death,
my eyes from tears, my feet from stumbling,
that I may walk before the LORD
in the land of the living.
—*Psalms* 116:8–9

To my niece, the real Skylar Grady,
you make me so proud to be your aunt!

ONE

Dying shouldn't be so difficult.

At least, in Skylar Grady's estimation it shouldn't be.

The way she saw it, if it were her time to die, she should be allowed to go quickly. No fuss. No muss. No wandering through the wilderness for days.

Her time to die?

No way did she plan for it to be that.

Then again, she hadn't planned to get lost in the Sonoran Desert, but there she was.

Lost.

She frowned, forcing herself to keep walking toward the shadowy mesa. A couple more miles and she'd be there. God willing, civilization would be on the other side. It better be, because six days with no food and minimal water had taken its toll. Much as she wanted to deny it, truth was truth. If she didn't find her way out soon, she wouldn't find her way out at all.

And that would be a shame. Not just because Skylar would be dead but because it also meant that the guy who'd drugged her, driven her out into the desert and left her to die would get away with it.

That definitely *wasn't* how Skylar planned for things to play out.

Unfortunately, she wasn't sure she had much of a choice in the matter.

Desert wilderness stretched out as far as the eye could see. No roads. No buildings. Nothing but an endless landscape of cacti and low-lying desert scrub, with the mesa in the distance. It's all she'd seen since she'd left her jeep, everything she had lived, breathed and felt for six days. She wanted out with a desperation that left her hollow and empty inside.

If there wasn't something or someone on the other side of the mesa…

She pulled her thoughts up short. Going there wouldn't help things. She had to keep walking, keep moving and, above all, keep hoping.

Lightning flashed in the distance, and the quiet rumble of thunder followed. Another storm. Was it the third or fourth since she'd made the decision to leave the rental jeep she'd woken in?

Did it matter?

Another winter storm meant water. Water meant life.

Her foot caught in thick desert scrub, and she fell hard, her breath leaving on a painful gasp. She forced herself up again, shivering as icy wind seeped through her T-shirt. Warm days. Cold nights. Sunburned skin and bone-deep chill. They'd taken their toll, and she wanted to rest more than just about anything.

But not more than she wanted to live.

Not more than she wanted justice.

And she *did* want that.

Someone had tried to kill her. She was going to find out who, she was going to find out why and she was going to smile when her would-be murderer was thrown in jail. First, though, she had to survive.

One trudging painful step after another to the mesa.

That was the only way to do it.

All around her, the night throbbed with energy and life; creatures moving in the darkness. Slithering, creeping, jumping creatures.

Were there wildcats in the desert?

Skylar didn't know, and she didn't want to find out.

Something shifted in the blackness, a deep shadow against the darkness. She blinked and it was gone, leaving nothing but a stillness that made the hair on the back of her neck stand on end. Something was out there. Something that was stalking her through the blackness. Skylar was as sure of that as she was of anything.

Something or some*one*.

Maybe the guy who'd left her to die had returned to make sure she'd done so.

She crouched low, not taking her eyes off the spot where the shadow had been, her hand skimming the ground. A weapon. Any weapon. That's what she needed.

But there was nothing.

No thick tree branches.

No heavy rocks.

She grabbed a fistful of dirt, her heart thumping a hard irregular beat, the desert pulsing with tension from something she couldn't see, but knew was there. Endless seconds passed, each moment a lifetime.

Please, God, let it be my imagination.

A figure appeared inches from where she crouched, stepping from blackness so suddenly Skylar was sure he'd disappear just as quickly.

She reached out, her fingers brushing a leather boot.

Real.

He was real.

"Skylar Grady?" His voice was smooth and deep, and Skylar didn't bother asking what he wanted. No way was this guy part of a search-and-rescue team. If he were, he wouldn't be alone. She jerked back, letting the handful of dirt fly before breaking into a sprint. Endless desert stretched out around her with no hope of rescue or safety. She knew it, but she ran anyway.

Please, Lord, get me out of this alive. Please.

Please.

Please.

The prayer chanted through her mind, matching pace with the frantic thrum of her pulse. Something snagged her shirt, pulled her back and she went fighting, swinging her fists the same way she had when she'd been a runty freshman in a high school overflowing with drug dealers and gang members.

"Cool it, Grady. I'm not in the mood to have my face beaten in." The command barely registered, and she swung again, her fist connecting with a rock-hard jaw.

"I said cool it." There was no heat in his words, and he grabbed her arm, pulling it behind her back with just enough pressure to hold her still.

"Let me go!" She stepped back, trying to unbalance him and loosen his grip, but he was as solid and unmoving as a mountain.

"I'm thinking your boss wouldn't be happy if I did that. Neither would I. I've lost and found your trail a dozen times these past couple days. I lose it again, and you may be lost for good."

"My boss?" She stilled, her heart beating too rapidly, her breath spilling out in great heaving gasps.

"Kane Dougherty. He's an old college friend. He called me the day before yesterday. Asked me to take part in the search-and-rescue operation that was launched to find you." His grip loosened, his hand smoothing up her arm and resting against her neck. "Take a deep breath, before you keel over."

"I'm not going to keel over." But she inhaled deeply, trying to force her racing heart to slow.

"I'm not sure I believe you. You've been out here for six days. That's a long time." His hand dropped away, and then he was in front of her, his eyes gleaming in the darkness.

"Long enough for people to stop looking for me. I haven't seen a search plane in two days, and then it was too far away to see me. I thought for sure I was going to have to find my own way out of here." She dropped onto the ground, relief making her light-headed.

Maybe she *was* going to pass out.

"They haven't stopped looking, they've just scaled back."

"Because they're looking for a body?" It made sense, but that didn't mean she wanted to hear it.

"It happens all the time. People drive into the desert to take pictures of the scenery, and they don't realize how unforgiving the terrain is. They get lost or hurt, and they run out of supplies."

"Look, buddy—"

"Jonas. Sampson."

"Look, *Jonas,* I didn't drive myself out here. Someone drove me. I didn't choose to go on a six-day sojourn. Someone else decided to send me on one."

"Who?"

"I don't know, but as soon as I get back to civilization, I plan to find out."

"You didn't see him?"

"I didn't see anything. I was out cold."

"Then, I guess the next question would be, 'Why?'"

"That's another thing I plan to find out once I get back to Cave Creek. So, how about we get in your jeep or truck or whatever you rode in on and get out of here?" She shivered, adrenaline fading and leaving her colder than she'd ever felt before.

"Sorry. No truck. No jeep. I track people on foot. Makes it easier to follow their trail."

"You're kidding, right?"

"No. Here." He crouched beside her, slid out of his backpack and pulled a jacket from it. "You'd better put this on. It's going to get a lot colder."

"Thanks." She put on the jacket, tried to zip it closed, but her hands were clumsy from too many days with no food.

"Let me." Jonas brushed her fingers away, his knuckles skimming her jaw as he pulled up the collar around her neck. Warmth lingered where his hands had been, and Skylar could feel it seeping into her.

Surprised, she shifted away, trying to see him through the blackness. Dark hair that was a little long and a little shaggy. High cheekbones. Eyes that could have been any color. He looked like an ancient warrior, and for a moment she wondered if she'd imagined the feel of boot leather, the conversation, even the scent of soap that hung in the air.

She reached toward him, realized what she was about to do and let her hand drop away.

"You okay?" he asked, and she nodded.

"Fine."

"Good. There's a storm blowing in, and we need to find shelter for the night." He offered a hand and pulled her upright.

"Five nights out here was plenty. How about we find shelter in town?"

"There's no way Phoenix Search and Rescue can send a helicopter for us until morning. No way we'll make it out on foot. Like it or not, we're stuck here until dawn."

"Then I guess we'll be walking all night, because there is no way I'm going to bunk down and accept my fate." She started walking, and Jonas pulled her to a stop.

"Even if we walk all night we won't reach the highway

before morning, and there's no way you're going to make it that long."

"I've been walking for days. One more night won't hurt me." Her teeth chattered on the last word, and she rubbed her hands up and down her arms. She felt cold to the bone, tired to the core. Every muscle in her body ached, but if it meant a hot meal, dry clothes and a warm bed, she'd walk all night.

"That's what most people probably think before the desert takes them."

"Nice, Jonas."

"I'm not nice. I'm realistic. You probably haven't eaten in a week and if you make it another mile, I'll be surprised. So, how about we do things my way? We head to the mesa, find some shelter and hunker down until first light." He handed her a water bottle, and she took a long swallow, letting the lukewarm liquid pour down her parched throat. Her hand shook as she wiped moisture from her lips, her stomach heaving in protest. Empty. That's what she was running on, and as much as she wanted to deny it, Jonas was right.

Her brain might be telling her to keep going, but her body was giving out. Quickly. As much as it aggravated her to depend on anyone, she'd have to follow Jonas's lead in this. "All right. Let's do this your way."

She didn't give him time to respond, just moved toward the mesa, hoping she didn't lose the water that seemed to be sloshing around in her empty stomach.

That's all she needed. Humiliation on top of exhaustion and pain.

"That was quick." His words rumbled through the darkness, a reminder that she might be cold and tired and sick, but she was not alone anymore.

That, at least, was something to be thankful for.

"What?"

"Convincing you to go along with my plan. Kane said you'd probably fight me tooth and nail on everything."

"Kane talks too much."

"That worked out well for you this time. If he hadn't told me that you were too stubborn to die, I wouldn't have agreed to help with the search." He didn't say what he must be thinking, what Skylar knew to be the truth. If not for Kane's intervention, she'd be facing another night alone in the desert. She might even be facing her *last* night alone in the desert. Her last night *period*.

She wasn't, though.

That was the important thing. Kane had sent help. Skylar would survive her trip to Arizona and her six-day hike through the desert. One more night. That's all she had to do, then she'd get a hot shower, a warm bed. Food. Her stomach rumbled loudly, the sound spilling out into the darkness.

"Hungry, huh?"

"What would make you say that?" She'd didn't hold back the snarky response, but maybe she should have. Jonas was, after all, her way out of the mess she was in. No sense getting on his bad side.

"Just a guess." He pulled something out of his pocket, barely breaking stride as he handed it to her. "Eat that, but take it slow. We don't have time to stop while you empty your guts."

"Your concern is touching." She glanced down at the protein bar, her mouth watering. Not a juicy burger, but she'd eat cardboard if it meant easing the gnawing hunger she'd been feeling for days. She tore the wrapper off, took the first bite and the second and the third.

Jonas grabbed the bar from her hand before she could take another.

"Hey!"

"I said take it slow. Not inhale it."

"If I were inhaling it, it would already be gone." She snatched the bar back, took another bite, actually managing to taste the nutty flavor before she swallowed. "It's good."

"I have more. I'll get them out when we stop."

"How about we stop now? Because I could eat another dozen of those." She licked crumbs from her fingers, thought about dragging Jonas to a stop and demanding whatever food he was carrying.

"Weren't you just saying you wanted to walk all night?"

"That was before I realized you had food."

"Three more miles and you can eat all the protein bars you want."

"Is that a bribe?"

"Whatever keeps you moving."

"More food would do it."

"Sorry. Everything else is in my pack. Getting it out would slow us down."

"Are we in a hurry?"

"Only if we want to beat the storm."

"I've weathered several storms already. One more won't kill me."

"The storm isn't the only thing I'm worried about." His pace had increased, and Skylar struggled to keep up, her sluggish movements no match for his long, easy stride.

"Please, don't tell me there are mountain lions out here. I really don't want to end up being cat food."

"Mountain lions aren't the worst predator we might run into. I've seen campfires the past couple nights. I thought members of the search party were following my trail, but the search-and-rescue coordinator said none of his people were out here."

"Maybe it's someone enjoying the desert," she offered, but she didn't believe it any more than she believed the person who'd drugged her and left her in the desert hadn't meant her any harm.

"That's what I thought, until you told me what happened to you."

"How far away were the fires?"

"A few miles the first night. Closer last night."

"So the people who built them could be right behind us."

"Could be."

"You're a man of few words, Jonas, and I find that truly annoying," she muttered, and he chuckled, the sound gritty and rough.

"I've never felt a need to waste words, but if you want me to expound on the kind of trouble we might be in, I will. You said someone drove you out here and left you—"

"I'm not just saying it. It happened."

"A person who goes to that kind of effort probably isn't going to sit around hoping that you're dead. Not when your face has been splashed on every local news station and not when every newspaper in the Phoenix area has been running stories on the search efforts."

"You think a killer is on our trail?"

"I think there's a possibility."

"In that case, walking three miles and getting to shelter isn't going to do us much good."

"Maybe not."

"So we could wait here. Ambush whoever is following. There's plenty of low vegetation. If we stay in the shadows—"

"No."

"What do you mean, no?"

"Exactly what I said."

"I didn't even finish outlining my plan."

"You don't have any breath or energy left to outline a plan, let alone ambush a posse."

"You never said a posse was following us."

"And I'm not saying it now. I'm just suggesting that you conserve your energy. You may need it before the night is over."

He was right.

Of course he was.

But for the first time in almost a week, she wasn't alone, and she was scared out of her mind that if she stopped talking, she'd be jerked back into reality and find herself lying on the desert floor. Alone again.

"I still think—"

"Shhhhhh." He slid his palm up her arm, his fingers curving around her biceps, the warning in his touch, in the subtle tensing of his muscles, doing more than words to keep her silent. She waited, ears straining as she listened for some sign that they weren't alone.

Thunder rumbled in the distance, and moisture hung in the air, carrying the musty scent of desert rain and wet earth. Nothing moved. No scurrying animals. No hum of life. Nothing but dead quiet, and a stillness that filled Skylar with dread.

A soft click broke the silence, and she didn't need to wonder what it was. She'd heard the sound hundreds of times during her days working as a New York City police officer.

She was on the ground before she could think, her body pressed against prickly plants and gravelly dirt, Jonas right beside her. Shoulder to shoulder, arm to arm.

She turned her head, met his eyes.

"Stay down," he whispered, the sound barely moving the air.

"That was a gun safety," she responded, trying to keep the words as quiet as his had been. Fear made them ring out louder than she'd planned, and he pressed a finger to her lips,

shook his head as he shifted, pulled something from beneath his jacket.

A Glock. 9 mm. Nice handgun. Exactly what she liked to
carry.

They weren't completely helpless, then.

He wasn't, at least.

She felt a split second of relief, and then Jonas was gone,
the darkness swallowing him so quickly, Skylar barely had
time to realize he was moving before he'd disappeared, and
she was alone again.

Alone, cowering on the desert floor, just waiting to be
picked off by an assassin's bullet.

No way. There was absolutely no way she was going to
die without a fight. She needed a better position, more cover.
She eased forward, her stomach scraping along the ground,
cactus needles and desert pebbles digging into her skin. A
minute passed as she struggled to move stealthily, her fa-
tigue-clumsy efforts loud in the silence, her thundering heart
masking any other sounds. Alone with her fear, wondering
if Jonas had been nothing more than a hallucination.

Alone like she'd been one too many times in her life.

Alone, and it was okay, because she would fight, and she
would win and she would get out of the desert alive.

She would.

A soft shuffle came from her left, and she stilled as a
shadow crept toward her. Short. Paunchy. Not Jonas. That's
all she saw. All she needed to see. She launched herself up
and toward him, her movements jerky and slower than she'd
intended. She realized her mistake too late to correct it, realized her own weakness as she barreled into the man's chest,
bounced backward, landed hard. Breath heaving, she barely
managed to dive to the left as the man aimed a pistol in her
direction, pulled the trigger. The bullet slammed into the
ground a foot from where she'd been, and she was up again.

Fight or die.

It was as simple as that.

Or, maybe, it was as simple as fight *and* die.

She didn't know.

Couldn't know, but she'd fight, anyway. It's what she'd done her entire life. No reason to give in now. Jonas was either real or he wasn't. He was somewhere nearby or not. God would intervene and save Skylar or He wouldn't.

One way or another, she'd fight.

She threw herself at the man's legs, knocking him off balance. A bullet whizzed past her shoulder. Then they were on the ground, tumbling into scrub and thorns, Skylar's overtaxed muscles trembling as she grappled for control of the pistol.

TWO

Shooting a moving target used to be easy.

Not anymore.

Now guns were the enemy; Jonas's memories of the damage they could do were as ripe and real as the nebulous mass that rolled on the ground ten feet away. Skylar and the man who'd been stalking them through the darkness. Jonas needed to aim his pistol, fire and hit one without hitting the other. A few years ago, he wouldn't have hesitated. Then he'd achieved sniper status with his band of Shadow Wolf brothers, his aim truer and more accurate than anyone on the team.

That was a lifetime ago, before his loss and his regrets.

He hadn't been to a target range in four years, hadn't fired a gun in just a little less than that.

Yet he was standing in the desert, holding his pistol as if he could still do what he'd done during his years as a border patrol agent.

Stop thinking about it, and do *something.*

Now!

He aimed, fired to the left of the struggling pair, the shot reverberating through the desert. One momentary explosion of sound, one small flash of light and then silence, the two heaving figures frozen in place. Skylar to the right. Her assailant to the left. An easy shot this time.

"Don't move, buddy. If you do, I guarantee it will be the last move you ever make. Where's his gun, Grady?"

"He dropped it while we were fighting." She panted, crawling through spiky desert foliage, coming up with the gun in her hand. "Got it."

"Good. Come over here. Let's give our friend a little space."

"I'd rather give him something else," she muttered, but she did as Jonas asked.

Surprising.

According to Kane, Skylar often fought for the sake of fighting. Tough and strong is how he'd described her. Jonas had still doubted that he'd find her alive. He had, and there was no going back and saying no as he had a hundred times since his wife and son were murdered.

No. I won't be coming back to work.

No. I won't help find the missing hiker, biker, photographer.

No, no, no.

This time he'd said yes. He'd committed to finding Skylar, and now he had to get her out of the desert alive.

"You got here just in time. That guy's pretty strong," she huffed, and he frowned.

"And you're pretty weak. I thought you were going to stay where I left you."

"I'm not the kind of gal who waits around for the cavalry to arrive. I'm surprised Kane didn't mention that while he was filling you in on my stubborn determination and charming nature." She started toward the perp, and Jonas tugged her back.

"He did. This time, though, the cavalry is here, and you are going to wait. I'll handle our perp." He didn't give her a chance to argue, just approached the gunman the way he'd done countless others, adrenaline pumping, gun drawn, all his focus on the potential threat.

"Face down. Keep your hands where I can see them." He issued the order, and then patted the prone man, found no other weapons. "He's clean."

"Let me go. You got no cause to do this to me."

"No cause? You tried to kill me." Skylar moved closer, crouched down beside the man, pressed the gun to his temple. "How about you tell me why?"

"There's nothing to tell. If I'd tried to kill you, you'd be dead." The man spat, his face pressed to the ground, his body still.

Jonas moved in, yanked him up by the arm as much to get him away from Skylar's gun as anything else. "How many people are with you?"

"Who said there's anyone with me?" His voice had a raspy smoker's edge, his braided hair falling over narrow shoulders. Old. Frailer than Jonas expected.

"How about we don't play games, old man? I saw your fire last night and the night before. You've been following me for a couple of days, and you're not alone. I want to know who is with you, and I want to know why you're after Skylar."

"I'm not after anyone. I'm out mindin' my own business, enjoyin' the desert. Nothin' wrong with that, is there?" He shifted, the subtle movement putting Jonas on edge. The desert had gone silent, the stillness more telling than any words the perp could have spoken.

"I think we'd better get out of here." He grabbed Skylar's hand, pulled her away from the old man.

"We can't just let him go. He tried to kill me." She pulled back, but he didn't release his hold.

"I want to survive the night. I want you to survive. If that means he escapes, so be it."

"But—"

"He's not alone, Grady. His friends could be anywhere, and I'm not willing to wait around for them to show up." Not only did he not want to wait around for them to show up, but he wanted to put as much distance between them and the perp as he could as quickly as he could.

Unfortunately, he wasn't sure how fast Skylar could move, how long she could keep going.

"I still think we should take him with us. I want answers. He's the only way to get them."

"Getting them won't do you any good if you're dead."

"I'm not planning on dying anytime soon."

"Most people aren't."

Gabriella hadn't been.

And Jonas hadn't been planning to lose her.

He shoved the thought aside, shoved aside the grief that went with it. He needed to focus on the moment, on the danger that followed them, on doing what he'd told Kane he would.

Find Skylar.

Get her back to civilization.

That was the mission. He'd fulfill it, then he'd go back to the life he'd built for himself. His woodworking shop, his job, the routine he'd forged in the months following Gabriella's death.

Nearly four years of routine.

It hadn't brought him peace, but it had brought him safety. No more heartache. No more sorrow. Nothing but restoring what had been left to decay. Old houses were easier to deal with than people.

Easier.

Safer.

Emptier.

"Do you think he's following us?" Skylar panted, pulling him back to the moment, the mission.

"He doesn't have a gun. We have two. I think he'll hang back and wait for his buddies to join him."

"I hope you're right, because I'm telling my legs to move, but they don't seem to be listening."

"You're doing fine." But he was nearly dragging her along, her stumbling steps keeping him from moving as fast as he would have liked. As fast as they needed to.

Somewhere in the distance a bird called, the sound crawling up his spine, urging him to hurry. Another call answered the first, and he tensed. He knew the desert and her creatures, and he knew the sound of a posse moving in, a net tightening. Knew it…felt it. If they didn't move fast, they'd be trapped, boxed in by the men who were hunting them.

"Kane said you're a marathon runner. Think you can turn on a little speed?"

"I—?" Skylar began, but he pulled her into a dead run, not giving her time to think, to doubt her ability. She had to know. Had to sense what he did. Danger breathing down their necks, nipping at their heels. Whatever she'd gotten involved in, it wasn't pretty, and if they weren't careful, it would take them both down.

"How much time do you think we have before they find us?" Skylar panted. A runner for sure, but a runner at the end of her reserves. How much farther could she go? How much more energy did she have to expend?

"Not enough," he answered her question and his own.

"I was afraid you were going to say that." She coughed on the last word, the sound tight and hot. Her hand was hot, too, heat coming off her body in waves. He could feel it through his sleeve.

The mesa was just ahead. A mile or less, but Skylar's pace was slowing, her breath coming in short, frantic gasps.

"We need to keep going, Grady. Another few minutes. You can give me that, right?" He tightened his grip on her hand, and she squeezed back, not bothering to waste breath responding.

Lightning flashed to the north, the low rumble of thunder reminding Jonas of another night, another woman. Pouring rain. Lightning. The sound of a gunshot. Gabriella falling, blood pouring from her chest. His frantic, futile attempts to staunch the flow as the storm raged around him.

He pulled his thoughts up short. The memories could still bring him to his knees if he let them. He wouldn't. Not now. Not when there was another life hanging in the balance, another woman depending on him.

Thunder rumbled again, and the first drop of rain fell on Jonas's cheek. A downpour would wash away their footprints, make it more difficult for their hunters to track them. More difficult, but not impossible. There were plenty of men in the area like Jonas, trained in the old ways and capable of finding the smallest trace of their prey.

"How much farther?" Skylar huffed, her words barely carrying above the sound of rain hitting the desert floor.

"We're almost there."

"Almost *where?*"

"The mesa."

"It's a sheer cliff, Jonas, a rock wall. We'll be trapped." She bit out the words one at a time, every ounce of her fear and anger ringing with them.

"It's not a sheer cliff, and we won't be trapped. Now, how about you save your energy for what lies ahead instead of wasting it on words?"

"Call me crazy, but when my life is hanging by a thread, I like to know the plan."

"The plan is we keep quiet, we keep going and we escape."

"We're about to run into a granite wall. Give me something more than that."

"You ever free-climb?"

"Not at night. Not in the rain. Not…" Her voice trailed off.

"What?"

"You're right. I need to save my energy." She clammed up; whatever she thought about climbing the mesa was her secret.

Jonas understood that.

He knew all about holding things close to the cuff, keeping them hidden, and he let silence take them both.

Thunder cracked, the sound reverberating through the darkness, the sudden, heavy downpour soaking through Jonas's shirt, dripping from his hair and into his eyes. There were ponchos in his pack, but he didn't waste time pulling them out. A dry corpse was just as dead as a wet one.

The rain drowned out any sound of pursuit, but Jonas's skin crawled, the hair on his nape standing on end. Danger was closing in.

Skylar must have sensed it, too. She tensed, her grip on his hand tightening, then loosening as she tried to pull free. "You go…ahead. I'll find a place to wait…and ambush our… followers."

"I didn't take you for a quitter, Grady."

"I'm not quitting, I'm—"

"Trying to make sure at least one of us survives? Because, if that's your plan, you'd better change it. I told Kane that I'd get you out of the Sonoran. That's what I'm going to do."

"One of us living is a whole lot better than both of us dying." She ground out every word deliberately as she yanked her hand away from his. She didn't stop running, though, and he pulled her up short as they reached the mesa, turned her to the east.

"This way." He knew the area well, had climbed the mesa dozens of times when he was a reckless teen searching for the next challenge. Had climbed it again as an adult seeking solace after the murders. The ridges in the rock face were as familiar as an old friend, and he slid his palm along the cool stone as he sought the large crevice that would lead them up.

There. Just under his fingertips. "This is it. There's a cave a hundred feet up. Ready?"

"I don't think I can do it." The words were barely a whisper, but Jonas heard the admission and the defeat.

"You don't have a choice."

"There are always choices. I can die with my feet planted on the ground, shooting it out and fighting. Or I can die trying to escape. I choose to fight."

"Who says trying to escape isn't fighting?" He pulled a rope from his pack. He hadn't bothered with full climbing gear, hadn't imagined he would need it. That had been his mistake. Hopefully, he wouldn't live to regret it. Wouldn't *die* regretting it.

"Me." She dropped onto the ground, pressing her face to her bent knees.

"Here's the thing, Grady." He crouched beside her, forced her chin up so they were eye to eye. "If you stay, I stay. That means I die, and I'm not willing to die tonight."

She stared into his eyes, rain streaming down her face, sopping her hair so that it clung to her head. She looked cold, tired, miserable, but she didn't look done. She looked angry. "How about you do your thing, and I do mine? How about you climb, and I stay?"

"How about we stop arguing and get moving?"

She hesitated, then stood. "Fine. We'll do it your way, but if I fall to my death, it's on your head."

"You won't fall." He tied the rope around his waist and hers, brushing her hands away when she tried to stop him.

"Says the man who hasn't been wandering around in the desert for six days," she muttered, but she was already reaching for the first handhold, already feeling her way around the lower edge of the wall, pulling up along the slippery rock, her muscles tight with effort, her face set.

A birdcall sounded through the storm, as out of place as a lion's roar in the city. Whoever followed had found their trail. It wouldn't be long before the hunter spotted the prey.

Hurry.

That's what he wanted to say, what he wanted to *shout* as he followed Skylar's slow ascent. Ten feet. Thirty. Fifty. Jonas could almost taste their victory, almost feel the relief that would come when he pulled himself over the ledge and into the cave.

Another birdcall and another.

Skylar slipped, her soft scream carrying above the storm. Jonas wedged his hand into a crevice, preparing to support her weight if she continued to fall. She slid another foot, then caught herself just above Jonas's position. He scrambled up beside her, pressing his free hand to her back, holding her steady as she caught her breath.

"I told you this was a bad idea," she mumbled, but there was no going back, and she knew it.

"We're almost there."

"This isn't a car ride through the country, Jonas. *Almost* may as well be a million miles away."

"A million mile journey begins—"

"With a single step. Right. How about we not get philosophical while we're hanging from the face of a cliff?"

"How about—"

"We keep moving?" She reached up, her fingers clawing at slick rock as she searched for a hold, found it, pulled herself onward with trembling arms. Below, a light jumped and swayed, the beam touching the base of the mesa before moving away.

Hurry, hurry, hurry.

The word chanted through Jonas's mind, but he didn't dare say it. Didn't dare push Skylar out of the slow, steady progress she was making. Almost done in, that's how she'd looked. There was a very fine line between that and done. Skylar had no choice but to move slowly, and Jonas had no choice but to follow. God willing, they'd make it. If not, at least they'd die trying.

The thought was cold comfort as Jonas moved into place beneath Skylar and started climbing again.

THREE

The rope loosened on Skylar's waist, and she knew Jonas was on the move. He seemed to easily navigate the same path she struggled with. No fear. No hesitation. If not for Skylar, he'd already be at the top of the mesa and moving away from the danger that stalked them. Instead, he stayed beneath her, matching her plodding pace. The weight of that, the responsibility of it, drove her on.

Rain poured from the sky, turning rough rock into slick ice. Too slick. One more missed handhold, one more slipped foot, and she'd go down, carrying Jonas with her.

Two bodies lying on the soaked desert floor.

She shuddered, reaching for the next handhold. She should have stayed on the ground. Should have insisted he go on without her, but he'd been right to think she wasn't a quitter. She'd never quit anything in her life, and she couldn't quit this. No matter how much her burning muscles might want her to.

"Come on, Grady, keep moving." Jonas's words penetrated her pain-induced fog, and she realized she'd stopped, was hugging the wall like she planned to stay there all night. Cold rain, throbbing heat, her body shaking with fatigue or fever or both, and all she could do was cling to her position and pray her cramped fingers didn't let loose, her trembling legs didn't give out.

"Climb!" Jonas shouted as if that would give her the impetus to move.

What he didn't seem to understand was that she wanted to move. She really did. But her body refused to cooperate. Her fingers dug deep into small niches, her feet pressed hard onto a tiny ledge of rock, and she could not move.

Could.

Not.

The rope slapped her hip as Jonas eased sideways and up. She didn't need to watch to know what he was doing. Moving into position to pass her.

No. Not pass.

He wouldn't leave her clinging to the mesa.

She hadn't known him long, but she knew that. Sensed it the same way she'd sensed trouble when she'd arrived in Cave Creek and started asking questions about the deadbeat dad she'd been tracking. Something had been brewing in the little town, and she should have turned tail and run. Instead, she'd dug in her heels, kept on asking, kept on pushing.

Someone had pushed back.

Who?

It was a question she'd been asking for the better part of a week. If she ever got out of the desert, she'd find the answer.

For now she needed to focus on surviving.

Focus on climbing.

Focus.

But her thoughts were as clumsy as her movements and scattered as easily as dry leaves on a windy day.

"Move it, Grady, because I'm not in the mood to toss you over my shoulder and carry you up to the cave." Jonas perched inches away, his eyes gleaming in the darkness.

"As if you could," she responded, the words slurred and thick, her teeth chattering on each one.

Not good.

She was losing it. She knew it. Jonas knew it. She could see it in his eyes, could sense it in the urgency of his words.

"I'll do what I have to do."

He would.

Of course, he would.

And they'd both die because of her.

Not the way she wanted to go. Not the end she'd imagined for her life, that was for sure. She'd much rather die an old lady, sitting in an easy chair reading a good book. Preferably after eating a very large and satisfying meal.

She scowled, reaching up, her muscles screaming in protest. Just a little farther. She could do that.

Please, God. Please, help me do it.

Jonas moved past her, the rope pulling tight on Skylar's waist. Seconds later, he called out from above.

"The rope is secure. Just another foot, and I can grab you and pull you into the cave." His words penetrated the thick haze that had wrapped itself around Skylar's brain. Another foot might as well have been a hundred, but she kept moving anyway, letting momentum carry her.

A hand wrapped around one wrist, grabbed the other as she reached again. Hard hands. Firm and warm. She had a split second to think those things, and then she was off the wall, lying on hard ground, staring up at blackness. No rain pouring down her face. No cold breeze biting through her borrowed jacket. No endlessly tall mesa to climb.

Nothing but darkness, and she slid into it, her eyes closing.

"Good job, Grady." The rough words echoed off the cave walls, and Skylar wanted to respond, but she had nothing left. No words. No energy.

A soft cloth wiped rain from her face, gentle hands tucked a Mylar blanket around her shivering body, a palm pressed to her forehead. "You're feverish."

Feverish?

Of course she was.

She had to be if she was letting someone take care of her.

The thought gave her enough energy to open her eyes, push onto her elbows. "I'm fine."

"You will be. Here." Jonas handed her two tablets and a bottle of water.

"What is it?"

"Something for the fever."

"I'm not much for taking medicine. I'll let the fever burn itself out." She thrust the medicine back, but he folded her fingers over the pills.

"It's a couple aspirin, Grady. It won't kill you, and it might make the night a little more comfortable."

She nodded, fumbling to open the water bottle. Aspirin she could do. It was other things she had to avoid. Hardcore painkillers had taken her mother twenty years ago, had almost taken Skylar seventeen years after that. She'd been a hair's breath from addiction in the months after she'd been shot and nearly killed in the line of duty. If not for Kane Dougherty, she might have chosen the path of least resistance, gone the way of her forefathers.

She owed him big for what he'd done.

Then again, he owed her big for sending her to Cave Creek and into a boatload of trouble.

She'd tell him as much once she made it back to civilization.

She yanked at the bottle top, scowling when it still refused to open. It was a water bottle, for goodness' sake. Not a combination lock. All she needed to do was twist, but her fingers were still clumsy from cold and exertion, and no matter how much she tried, she couldn't manage the simple task.

"Let me." Jonas eased the bottle from her hand, opened it, then returned it, his fingers brushing her knuckles, the contact spreading warmth through her chilled skin. She wanted to lean close, let his heat seep into her icy body. Instead, she took a swig from the bottle to help swallow the aspirin, pulled the Mylar blanket close, trying to stave off the tremors that racked her body.

"Thanks."

"Maybe you should save the thanks for after I get you to the airport and on the plane back to New York."

"That might take a while, seeing as how I have a score to settle and I'm not leaving town until I do it." She took another sip of water, pulled the gun from her waistband and set it on the ground. She had firepower, *and* she wasn't alone. She'd managed to free-climb the mesa without falling to her death.

Things were definitely looking up.

"It might not take as long as you think. I have express orders to get you out of the desert and onto the next plane back to New York."

"Funny, you don't seem like the kind of guy who takes orders."

"Depends on who is doing the ordering. When it's a good friend who's concerned about his employee, I'm willing to go along with the plan."

"Unfortunately, *I'm* not." She set the water bottle on the ground, tried to see Jonas's face through the darkness. She had the sense of harnessed energy and restrained strength, of corded muscle and irritation. He'd come to her aid, and he expected her to want to be rescued.

And she did.

From the wilderness. From her six-day nightmare, but

not from her obligation to follow up on the case she'd been investigating. Certainly not from her obligation to find the person who'd tried to kill her.

Was *still* trying to kill her.

"You may not have a choice, Grady. You're done in. Sticking around town, searching for answers when you're sick and exhausted could get you killed."

"Not if I'm careful."

"Were you being careful when someone knocked you out and drove you out into the desert?"

"How about we have this argument after we're back in civilization?"

"Avoiding the question doesn't change the answer."

"And asking it doesn't change my mind. I'm sticking around until I figure out who wants me dead and why."

"Kane said you were stubborn."

"I see that as one of my better qualities."

"Good to know." He chuckled, the sound rusty and dry.

"You should also know that after we get out of here, I'm planning on doing things my way. No trip to New York. No hiding away while someone else solves my problems."

"We'll see." He moved away, leaving her shivering under the Mylar blanket.

"Where are you going?"

"Just checking on our friends."

"Do you really think you'll be able to spot them?" She pulled the blanket around her shoulders and followed him to the mouth of the cave. Rain blew in on a gust of air, and her teeth chattered, but she was not going to lie on the floor of the cave while Jonas did what she should be doing herself.

"Maybe."

"And you're sure they found our trail?" She peered out into the darkness, seeing nothing but gray-black night.

"Yes."

"I'd ask you why, but you'd probably just say 'because.'"

He chuckled again. "They followed my trail for at least two days. I don't think they'll have any trouble following it here."

"The rain might have washed our tracks away."

"Possibly, but they'll know we were heading this way, and the only thing here is the mesa."

"So, they could be on their way up."

"Not with the storm still raging and not until they know for sure where we climbed."

"So, we're safe until the rain stops."

"Safe enough for you to lie down and rest."

"I don't need rest. I need answers. I came to Arizona to find a deadbeat dad who owed twenty thousand dollars back child support. Now I'm running for my life. I want to know why." She stared out into the darkness, rain splattering her face, icy against her overheated skin.

"Could be the dad doesn't want to pay up."

"And decided to commit murder to avoid it?"

"People have committed murder for less reason."

"True, but not this time. My brain might not be functioning on full capacity, but it's still working well enough for me to know that. I hadn't even found the guy. He had no reason to think I would. He ran from New York two years ago. Ran from Chicago seven months ago. Every time the police close in on him, he runs. Why stop running now?"

"Good question, but you won't find your answer tonight. Come on." He led her back into the depth of the cave, urged her to lie down again.

She wanted to protest.

Couldn't.

Her body felt leaden, her legs weak, and all she could do was exactly what he wanted—lie down, close her eyes, sink into darkness.

He brushed sopping hair from her cheek, felt her forehead again, and she let him. Let him take care of her in a way she hadn't let anyone take care of her in a very long time.

She didn't like it, felt helpless to do anything else.

Jonas lifted her head, slid his pack beneath it and she opened her eyes, looked into his face.

"Who are you, Jonas Sampson?" she asked, the question stumbling out without thought.

He hesitated, the shrugged. "Just a friend of your boss."

"Kane wouldn't have called in someone who was just a friend to do this job."

"No. I guess he wouldn't have. Get some sleep, Grady. We may have a long night ahead of us. I'm going to see if I can get some reception and call for transport. With any luck, we'll have a ride out of here by first light." He moved away, and she didn't have the strength to say what she was thinking.

It would take more than luck to get a ride out before the enemy closed in. It would take skill, determination, faith.

Faith.

That illusive thing that she clung to with both fists, but that always seemed to slip from her grasp when the going got tough. She'd beg for help but instead of waiting for an answer, she'd jump in to solve the problem herself. Head-first, not even looking to see where she might land.

She'd learned her lesson about depending on others early, and she'd learned well. A drug-addicted mother, an alcoholic father, no one she could really trust to help her when she'd needed it—those things had made her the person she was. Maybe that's why she constantly struggled for control, tried to call the shots when she should really be allowing God to lead the way. Jumped into things without a firm plan in mind.

Any way she cut it, the results were always the same. Trouble.

And she was in it again.

This time, she had no choice but to depend on God.

Depend on Jonas.

A stranger who'd stepped in and offered help she desperately needed.

A stranger she could trust with her life?

She hoped so, because the darkness she'd been holding at bay was closing in, her hold on the world was slipping and she was falling into dreams and nightmares and memories.

She jerked upright, afraid to let go, afraid of what it would mean if she woke and Jonas was gone and she was there, alone in a cave a hundred feet above the ground.

"Hey, calm down, everything is okay." He was at her side, pressing her back before she could stand.

"No. It's not. I'm out in the middle of nowhere, running for my life with a man I don't know."

"You know Kane, and you know the kinds of friends he keeps. Isn't that enough?" The question seeped in, eased her frantic thoughts.

He was right.

She did know Kane.

She did know the kind of friends he kept.

Good people, all of them.

But she still didn't want to let go, didn't want to give in.

She tracked Jonas's movement as he walked back to the mouth of the cave, watched as he settled there, cross-legged, watching the desert floor, doing what she should be doing herself.

What she couldn't do herself.

She didn't like it.

She didn't like it at all, but darkness edged in anyway, stole her thoughts, her fears, her need for control, and she couldn't fight it, couldn't stop it as it swept her away.

FOUR

Jonas had been prepared for a lot of things when he'd headed out to find Skylar. Days trekking through the desert, nights in subfreezing temperatures, an injury victim, maybe even a body. What he hadn't prepared for was a posse of armed men.

But that's what he'd gotten.

He'd have a few words to say to Kane when he made it back to civilization.

If he made it back.

The way things were looking, he might not.

Rain still fell heavy and constant, the thick clouds and poor weather preventing Phoenix Search and Rescue from coming to their aid. That left Jonas and Skylar to find their own way out of the trouble they were in. He was up to the task. He wasn't so sure about his companion. She hadn't moved in the past hour, her body curled into a fetal position, her head resting on his backpack.

She was tough, he'd give her that.

As tough as Kane had said.

But even the toughest people had their breaking point, and he thought Skylar might have reached hers. Feverish and weak, she'd barely managed to make it to the cave. Sheer grit had carried her the last dozen feet. Maybe sheer grit would see her the rest of the way out of this mess.

Maybe.

He couldn't count on it, though.

And he wouldn't leave her behind.

He'd come to the desert with a mission—find Skylar Grady and bring her back to civilization.

He'd leave the desert with her, or he wouldn't leave it at all.

In the first weeks and months and even years following Gabriella's murder, the thought of failing might have had a tantalizing ring. Death seemed like a friend when life became the enemy. He'd survived that first wave of grief and self-loathing. Slowly, he'd come to accept that life could go on without his wife and son.

Could go on. Did go on. But it could never be the same again. *He* couldn't be the same, couldn't be the man he once was.

So, he went on with it, drifting from old house to old house, refinishing, rebuilding, creating beauty from decay.

Too bad he hadn't been able to do that with his life. Create something new from the ruins of what had been. Something meaningful out of something senseless.

"Are they on the move?" Skylar's voice carried through the darkness, scratchy and raw, breaking through thoughts that were just as raw, just as scratchy.

"You're supposed to be sleeping." He glanced her way, saw that she was moving toward him, the blanket crinkling as she pulled it close.

"It's hard to sleep when death is knocking on your door."

"He's not knocking, yet. Go back to sleep." He turned his attention back to the desert floor. Dark and empty of life, it was shadowed with night, the thick winter foliage offering shelter to anything or anyone who might want to hide there.

"You know I'm not going to do that, right?" Skylar dropped down beside him, Mylar crunching and crackling.

"I guess I do."

"And I guess you know I'm going to ask until I get an answer. *Are they on the move?*"

"Things look quiet."

"But?"

"They don't feel quiet. My gut is saying that company is coming."

"A person should never ignore his gut. I think we need to get out of here. Come on." She rose, but he grabbed her hand, holding her in place.

"Moving quickly and without a plan won't do either of us any good."

"Sitting around waiting to be killed won't, either." But she settled down beside him again.

"That was easy." Surprised, he studied her face, tried to read her expression.

"Lately, I've been thinking that I should spend a little more time planning before I jump into things. Now is as good a time as any to start."

"Glad to hear it."

"Yeah, well, when a life is on the line, I can't afford to make foolish mistakes."

"*Lives.* Last time I checked, there were two of us in this cave."

"True, but your life is the one I'm worried about. I made my own mess. If I die because of it, it'll be my own fault. If you die…" Her voice trailed off, but she didn't need to continue for him to understand.

He knew all about guilt. Had felt it every minute of every day for four years.

"It won't be your fault. It will be the fault of the men who are after us."

"The men who are after *me*. You're an innocent bystander in this."

"I'm a willing participant, and I assume all risk and responsibility for myself."

"You wouldn't be here if I'd done what I should have and asked Kane to send backup as soon as I realized something about the case was off."

"Off?" A shadow moved a hundred yards out, and Jonas tracked it. Human, animal or simply a product of rain and wind and shifting foliage? He couldn't be sure, but his gut said that the trouble they'd been waiting for was about to find them.

"The guy I came to find? He supposedly left town a week before I arrived. Thing is, he was still getting mail at his house. His truck was still in the driveway."

"Could be he got a new ride. One that couldn't be traced to him."

"Could be, but people in Cave Creek seemed awfully closemouthed about a guy who'd only been in the area for a few months."

"Small towns are notorious for protecting their own."

"He wasn't theirs."

"Maybe not, but he belonged there more than you did." The shadow moved again, and this time there was no doubt.

Human.

For sure.

Moving stealthily, keeping low.

Skylar tensed, and he knew she'd seen what he had. Danger closing in. "Your instincts were right. Now are you ready to get out of here?" Skylar stood again, and Jonas followed, grabbing his pack and pulling out extra ammo.

"What I'm ready to do doesn't matter. What matters is what you're capable of doing."

"You don't think I can climb out of here?" She lifted the

gun she'd left near his pack, held it like it was part of her hand, part of her.

"How good of an aim are you?"

"You're avoiding the question," Skylar noted.

"And asking my own. How about we don't waste time with verbal sparring?"

"I'm good. I was better before I left the force, but I still go to the range for target practice. You never know when being a crack shot could come in handy."

"Wish I'd been thinking that way over the past few years," Jonas remarked.

"You were a police officer?"

"Border patrol, but that was a lifetime ago."

"How long of a lifetime?"

"Nearly four years." He scanned the area below the mesa. The shadow had disappeared, fading into the rest of the landscape, but Jonas had no doubt the person was still there, still coming. And he wasn't alone. There'd been other shadows moving in the past hour. Other furtive advances on the desert floor.

"That's not so long. I've been out of the force for three." She might have been making idle conversation, but Jonas sensed a change in her, a tension that spoke of the same need for action he felt.

"No, I guess it's not." And he guessed he hadn't forgotten how to hold a gun, how to use it. Hadn't forgotten the way adrenaline felt coursing through his body, the way every nerve ending came alive during the waiting and during the hunt.

Hadn't forgotten.

Had maybe even missed it.

"You said we needed a plan. I think now is as good a time as any to come up with one, because that feeling you have?

I've got the same one. Things are about to get ugly, and I'm not sure I want to be around when they do."

"Go back in the cave and rest. If they start climbing, I'll start shooting. If I need backup, I'll call for it."

"*That's* your plan?" She sounded so disgusted Jonas would have smiled if the situation hadn't been so serious.

"It's that or climb, and I don't think we're in any condition to do that."

"You don't think *I'm* in any condition to climb, you mean."

"Same thing."

"How many people do you think are out there?" She didn't argue, just lifted the rope from the place where he'd dropped it.

"I've counted at least seven. Probably closer to a dozen."

"A dozen? I guess I really did make some friends in Cave Creek." She ran a hand over her hair, staring down into the desert as if she could read it and the secrets it held.

"We're both good shots. I have extra ammo. We'll be fine."

"Not if they have high-powered rifles and night vision. We start shooting, we give away our location. They'll start shooting. There's a good possibility the bad guys won't be the only ones who die. We're going to have to go with Plan B aka, my plan. We climb."

"Grady—"

"To take a page from your book, how about we don't waste time with verbal sparring? I can make it, but not if I spend too much time thinking about it." She tied the end of the rope around her waist, tossed the other end to Jonas.

He could argue, or he could do what he'd been wanting to do for the better part of an hour—get out while he still could. Another fifty feet, and they'd crest the top of the mesa. Fifty feet wasn't far. Not for a good climber, and Skylar obviously was one.

What she wasn't, was healthy.

"It's fifty feet, Grady. Up wet rock, in the dark. And it's a long way down. We could both die."

"We could both die, anyway, so I'm willing to take the chance. Besides, you didn't seem all that worried when we had to climb a hundred." She grabbed the end of the rope from his hand, leaned close to knot it around his waist.

"I was. I'm just good at hiding my feelings."

"I'll keep that in mind." She patted his cheek, her palm hot and dry, and he captured her hand, holding it when she would have pulled away.

"What are you planning, Grady?"

"An escape." But there was something in her tone that didn't ring true.

"And?"

"You go first. I'll follow."

"I don't think so." There was no doubt in his mind that she'd stay behind, stand her ground and fight until she was shot.

Blood spurting from a bullet wound to the chest, spilling out and over his hands.

He pulled his thoughts up short, refusing the memory as he checked the knot on Skylar's end of the rope and then on his own.

"There are handholds carved into the rock to the left of the cave opening. First one is at foot level." The notches had been carved thousands of years ago and had been used by native peoples for generations. For those who knew they were there, they were easy to find.

For others, the way up was more of a struggle.

Skylar slid her foot out, scrambled to find a notch. The rain had slowed, but it still fell, making the going more treacherous, the chance they were taking less certain.

He needed to call her back, tell her to forget it.

His plan would have to work.

He'd make it work.

There was no other choice. He couldn't live with the knowledge that he'd failed to save someone who depended on him.

Not this time.

Not again.

Before he could stop her, she found her footing and climbed out into the rain, the rope tugging against his waist as she moved up and away. At least they had that. If she slipped, he might be able to keep her from falling, the rope between them a safety line that could keep her alive.

Her legs disappeared. Her feet. The rope tugged again, and then dropped, puddling near his feet and slithering over the edge of the cave.

She'd untied herself.

Weak, shaky and without a safety line, one missed hand-hold, one slipped foot, and she'd fall to her death.

Blood pooling onto the ground, life spilling out.

He moved out onto the rock ledge, his heart slamming against his ribs, fear and fury driving him on. He should have realized what she'd planned. Should have known she wouldn't do things his way. Not if it meant she might pull him down with her.

He climbed until they were side by side, her trembling body just a few feet to his left. "Are you crazy!"

"I think we both are," she panted, her breathing barely controlled.

"Focus, Grady. You lose your breath, you'll lose your grip. Hold your position so I can tie your safety line."

"Too dangerous. Just keep going."

"Climbing without a safety—"

"Jonas, shut up and climb, okay? Because I do not have the strength to do what I'm doing *and* argue with you." She pulled up another few inches, found a handhold and kept moving.

He followed, his gaze dropping to the desert floor. A hundred and thirty feet to rocky soil and certain death. He couldn't let her fall. Couldn't allow her to lose focus.

He stayed silent, following her up inch by agonizing inch. No sign of their pursuers yet, but it was only a matter of time before someone looked up and saw them perched on the rock face.

One shot from a high powered rifle and Skylar would be dead.

Blood spilling out.

Not this time. Please, God. Not this time.

The prayer caught him by surprise. His faith had been so used up, so dried out after the murders, that he'd made no attempt to regain it. Had missed it only in a peripheral way. Church had become an empty ritual he did to assuage his family's worries. Sermons were just words printed on a heart that was too hardened to acknowledge them.

God was too far to reach, too big to care.

And Jonas hadn't cared, either.

Until now.

Now he wanted desperately to believe that the faith of his childhood was real and alive. That God could and would reach down and lend a hand.

His fingers slipped on wet rock, his left foot sliding from its mooring. He forced himself to keep calm as he anchored himself again. Ascended another few feet.

Losing focus was a sure way to die, and, if he died, Skylar might, too. He moved up another dozen feet, the cold air ripping through his shirt. Beside him, Skylar eased to the left. Up. To the right. Up. Slowly, surely, making progress.

Maybe they'd make it to the top.

And maybe the God who'd seemed so far away for so long was only a prayer away.

Neither seemed likely, but Jonas forged on anyway, his knee-jerk prayer whispering through his mind, sinking into his soul as he pushed on toward the top of the mesa.

FIVE

Just a little farther.

Just a little more.

One more push.

One more pull.

One more pain-filled gasping breath.

One.

More.

The only problem was, Skylar wasn't sure she had one more of anything to give. Not a push, a pull or a breath.

She anchored herself to the mesa, trying to ease the pressure on her burning arms and hands, her forehead pressed to cold, wet stone.

Pack things up and keep going. That's the way to do things. You stay too long in one place, and you'll die there.

Her sister's, Tessa's, voice seemed to whisper through the darkness, and Skylar could imagine her clinging to the mesa, black hair blowing in the wind, her pale face filled with mischief. It had been nearly fifteen years since Tessa had walked out of their childhood home and left Skylar to deal with their father alone. Fifteen years since Skylar had seen or spoken to her, but the voice seemed as real as if they were both still standing in the living room of their father's double-wide trailer.

"You okay?" Jonas maneuvered into place beside her, his movements effortless. No doubt he was furious about the untied rope, but it didn't show. Nothing showed but his determination to get them both to the top.

"Fine." Except that her arms were going to fall off, her legs give out and she was going to tumble to her death. At least she wouldn't carry him with her.

"Then prove it. Finish what you started." No pity, no sympathy, no encouragement. Just a barked command for Skylar to do what she had to do.

"How much farther?" She ground out the question as she reached for the next handhold, her heart pulsing a strange uneven rhythm. She felt light-headed, her limbs no longer hers, and she bit the inside of her cheek, trying to force adrenaline back through her body.

"Twenty feet."

Twenty?

It felt like she'd already climbed a thousand.

Her body shook with effort as she struggled up. Close. So close to victory. She could almost taste it. Almost feel the cold wet earth beneath her overtaxed body.

"Hold tight." Jonas shot out the command, and Skylar followed it, her breath heaving, her lungs burning, fingers clinging tight to slick rock. She glanced down. Way down. Was sure she saw shadows moving.

"Hurry." She wanted to shout the request, but it emerged as a whisper that even she could barely hear.

And then he was reaching down, his hands hooking around her wrists, pulling her up and over so quickly she barely felt the scrape of stone against her stomach, barely realized she was moving before she was lying on the ground, gasping, coughing, nearly crying with relief.

"Don't ever play a game like that with me again, Grady. Is

that clear?" Jonas growled as he pulled her to her feet, held her arm while she caught her balance.

"I don't play games," she managed to say, the pain in her arms and legs nearly doubling her over. She stood her ground, though. Didn't back down. She'd done what she had to do. Made sure that at least one of them would survive.

"What do you call this?" He yanked the rope from his waist.

"My way of making sure I didn't die knowing that I was taking someone else to eternity with me."

"A selfish choice. Come on. We need to move before we lose our lead." He stalked away, and she followed, her legs trembling with the aftermath of her climb.

"Selfish? I was trying to save your life."

"So that I could live knowing I couldn't save yours?"

"It wasn't your job to save my life. It was your job to find me. You did."

"It's my job to get you out of the desert and back to New York. That's what Kane asked me to do. It's what I intend to do. Do us both a favor. Stop being so pigheaded, and let me."

"Has anyone ever told you that you're rude?"

"More times than I can count."

"And it hasn't occurred to you that it's something you need to work on?"

"It's occurred to me." He eased the pace, slowing from a brisk walk to a leisurely stroll as if they had all the time in the world. They didn't, but Skylar wasn't capable of much more than the new pace he'd set. He knew it. Of course he did. Jonas didn't seem like the kind of guy who missed things. Not bad guys lurking in shadows. Not noises in the darkness. Certainly not Skylar's limping pace and panting breath.

"It's occurred to *me* that I'm slowing you down. You got me up the mesa. You really don't have to stick around. The guys who are after us are really only after *me,* and as much as I want to swoon like a Victorian lady and let you carry me out of the desert on your manly shoulders, I don't want your blood on my hands."

"Manly shoulders?"

"My point is—"

"I know what your point is, Grady. Here's mine. I watched my wife and unborn son die a few years ago. I was helpless to save either of them. I'm *not* helpless to save you. All the arguments you throw out? They're not doing anything but wasting energy. Yours *and* mine." His words stopped her cold, and she touched his arm, felt corded muscle beneath wet cotton.

"I'm sorry. I can't imagine anything more painful than that."

"It was…tough."

An understatement. Skylar knew that.

Not her business, but she wanted to ask how they'd died. Why. Wanted to tell him again how sorry she was.

"Jonas—"

"There's a path to the desert floor on the north side of the mesa. Not too steep. If we're careful, we should be able to make it down without a problem." He cut her off, his tone gruff.

"As long as we're not hanging off the face of a rock again, I'll be happy." She tripped, nearly tumbling face-first onto the ground.

"Like I said, we need to be careful." He wrapped an arm around her waist, urging her on. Warmth spread through her at the contact, the heat of his arm seeping through layers of wet cloth, making her want to burrow close, steal more of his warmth. She moved away instead, uncomfortable with her need, her weakness.

Rain dripped down her hair and into her eyes, but she

didn't bother wiping it away. It was too dark to see much anyway, and she was too tired to do more than keep trudging across the mesa. They were on the path before she realized it, and Jonas stepped in front of her, his movements as lithe and fluid as a jungle cat.

"We'll have to go single file. I'll go first. You follow. Stay close." He snagged both her hands, pressing them to his waist, and her fingers twisted through his belt loops. She didn't protest, or try to pull away. As much as she didn't want him to die because of her, she wanted to survive. He was her lifeline. It was as simple as that. As frustrating as that. She'd spent most of her life clawing and fighting to prove that she could make it on her own, and now she had no choice but to admit she couldn't. Without Jonas, she'd die. The wind, the rain, the cold, all sapped her strength, made her clumsy, every step an effort in concentration, every movement sluggish and difficult.

A voice carried on the wind. Or maybe it was simply her imagination. Either way, she wanted to move faster. Her foot caught on a rock, and she stumbled, falling into Jonas's back, her head slamming into his pack. She saw stars, felt reality slipping away. No more rain or cold or wind. Just easy darkness and silence and warmth. All she had to do was let herself go.

"I thought you weren't going to make me sling you onto my manly shoulders and carry you out of here." Jonas's voice pulled her back from the brink of unconsciousness. He'd wrapped his arms around her so they were pressed close, his warmth seeping through her chilled body, his arms supporting her deadweight. She tried to push away, but he held her head to his chest. "Just take a minute."

"A minute isn't going to do me any good, but thanks for the offer." She tried to keep her voice light, hoped he didn't hear her desperation.

"I did search and rescue for a lot of years," he said, letting her go and walking again.

"Yeah?"

"There were plenty of times when a person I thought was equipped to survive, someone who was trained in survival or used to the environment, didn't make it. There were even more times when someone who wasn't prepared at all, someone I was sure I'd find dead, pulled through."

"The will to survive is a powerful thing." She snagged his belt loops again, trying to concentrate on his words, hoping to clear her head, sharpen her thinking.

"It is, but, all things being equal, the difference between survival and death doesn't lie in the will to live. It lies in the ability to hope. Once hope is lost, everything else is lost with it."

"Don't worry. I have plenty of hope. I'm just running short on steam."

"I have granola and raisins in my pack. A few more protein bars. Probably a couple apples, too. I'll get them out once we're on flat terrain. For now we need to keep moving." He didn't say why, didn't mention their pursuers, but Skylar could feel the hot breath of the hunter on her neck, could imagine high-powered rifles aimed at her. At any moment, a bullet could slice through the darkness, slam into her back.

The wind abated, the rocky landscape giving way to thick scrub as the slope eased.

Solid ground beneath her feet.

Finally.

Skylar would have knelt and kissed the desert floor if she'd thought she could make it back to her feet again.

"You did good, Grady." Jonas didn't slow as he pulled off his pack, dug into it and handed her an apple.

"And this is my reward?"

"Would you rather have a medal?"

"Maybe." She bit into the apple because she needed the fuel, not because she felt hungry. All she felt was exhaustion, pulling at her, slowing her down. Maybe the apple would help. Probably, it wouldn't.

The difference between survival and death doesn't lie in the will to live. It lies in the ability to hope.

The words drifted through her mind. Jonas's words. Tessa's voice. She glanced around, almost expecting to see her long-lost sister somewhere nearby.

They'd been opposites growing up. Skylar the pragmatist. Tessa the optimist, always filled with dreams and hopes for the future. Foolish dreams, in Skylar's mind, but she'd never had the heart to tell her sister that. Maybe, secretly, she'd wanted to believe all those hopes and dreams would come true for both of them. Maybe she *still* wanted to believe they would.

She frowned, taking another bite of the apple because she was seriously afraid she was losing her mind.

"Here." Jonas dropped something over her head, pulled it into place around her neck.

"What is it?" She ran her fingers along a thin leather cord, several cold beads and what felt like a stone arrowhead.

"Your medal."

"It feels like an arrow."

"One of my grandfather's. His grandfather taught him how to make them. He taught me. Better than anything you could buy in a store. At least, that's what he always said. Me? I was more into bullets than bows, but he wanted me to remember the old ways, so he gave me that for my sixth birthday."

"I can't take it, then." She started to pull it off, but he stilled her hands.

"You earned it. Besides, Pops gave me a few every year until I was thirteen and could make them myself. I used to earn money selling them at a gift store outside the reservation."

"An entrepreneur at a young age, huh?"

"A kid who didn't value what he had but, then, what kid does?"

Not Skylar.

Not that she'd had much to put value in.

A drug-addicted mother. An alcoholic father. A wild older sister. A cluttered, unstable home. School had been her refuge, and she *had* valued that. But family had always been a distant dream. One she still hadn't reached. "I still don't feel comfortable taking it."

"You're not taking. I'm giving."

"You're splitting hairs."

"And you're fighting me again."

"It's better than thinking about how many hours there are until dawn and how tired I am."

"Not so many left, Grady. It's almost two, and the rain is letting up. I put a call in to search and rescue while you were sleeping. They know our situation. As soon as the storm clears, they'll send a chopper."

If they survived that long.

She didn't say what she was thinking. Just kept walking, her gaze focused on the dark horizon. No lights. No sign of civilization. Nothing but exactly what she'd been seeing for days. "You know, I've spent the past six days heading toward the mesa, hoping civilization was on the other side. There's nothing here, though. Just more desert."

"It's a big place. Easy to get lost in."

"But you know where we're headed."

"Right now we're just headed away from what's behind us."

"How much lead time do you think we have?" Her words

were raspy, her throat hot. *Everything* was hot. Her face, her hands, her entire body, burning from the inside out.

"Hopefully, enough."

"That doesn't sound very promising." She glanced over her shoulder, scanning the mesa. A shadow moved along the top. Two shadows. Three. Her pulse leaped, and she nearly stumbled. "They're on the mesa."

And she was deadweight, slowing Jonas down. "I think—"

"Don't waste your breath. We're together, and we're staying together."

"Then we need to move faster."

"And risk you not being able to move at all? I don't think so."

"But—"

"If they had night vision and high-powered rifles, they'd have picked us off long ago. Since they don't, they'll need to climb down the mesa. Once they're down here, we're on an equal playing field. No way will they be able to see us. That means they'll need to track us. That means time."

"And they have plenty of that."

"A few hours. That's not much."

"It's an eternity." Sweat trickled down Skylar's forehead, heat consuming her, sapping what little energy she had. She raised a hand to brush it away, her arm shaking. A week ago, she'd been strong and fit and ready to conquer Cave Creek, Arizona. Now she felt two hundred years old, her body aching and weak. It brought back memories she preferred not to dwell on. Those dark days in the hospital when doctors had stood over her bed and shaken their heads as she'd insisted that she'd walk again.

She'd beaten the odds then.

Maybe she'd beat them again.

But it didn't seem likely just now.

They hit the crest of a small hill, and she glanced over her shoulder, saw shadows weaving their way down the mesa.

Her foot caught on a rock, and she flew forward, her legs going out from under her so quickly she didn't have time to try to recover. She landed with a thud, skidding a few feet forward, the breath knocked from her lungs.

Get up.

Get.

Up.

Her mind screamed the command, but her body refused to listen.

"You okay?" Jonas crouched beside her, not touching her, not trying to hurry her to her feet. Just waiting. He'd brought them across flat ground, up a hill and was ready to lead them down the other side and out of the sight of their pursuers.

She just had to get back on her feet and go.

Easy.

She scowled, pushing away from the rocky earth, her palms stinging as she levered onto her knees, struggled to her feet, ignoring the hand Jonas offered.

"Let's go." Her knees stung, and she was sure her jeans had ripped. Thought her skin had ripped, too, but she didn't have time to check for damage.

"You need to stop looking back, Grady. It'll trip you up every time." Jonas spoke quietly, and she didn't respond.

What would she say?

That being tripped up by what was behind her was the story of her life? That she'd spent so much time looking back that she'd forgotten to look forward, and that she'd traveled from New York City to Cave Creek, Arizona, hoping that a change of scenery would help put an end to her days of mourning what could have, should have, *would* have been, if only she hadn't been such a fool?

She frowned, turning her attention back to where it

needed to be, taking one step after another after another. One breath after another. One heartbeat. Until all she knew was the movement, the pain and the soft sound of the rain hitting the earth.

SIX

Dawn broke as they neared a damp creek bed, the first watery rays of sun so welcome, Skylar would have cried if she'd had any energy left for it.

They'd made it through the night.

Made it through mile after mile of endless walking.

Made it.

"Thank You, God," she whispered.

"Don't thank Him, yet. We still have to survive until our ride gets here."

"How long do you think that will be?" Because Skylar was done. More done than she'd ever been in her life. Sheer determination had kept her going through the long night. That and Jonas. But the storm had ended, the sun was rising and so was the feeling that she couldn't take another step, that her battered, pain-filled body couldn't go another minute.

No matter how much she wanted it to.

"The storm broke less than an hour ago. The sky is mostly clear. I'd say they'll be here in the next hour."

"How about calling and telling them that we're ready now?" she asked, only half joking. She felt parched and sick, her vision blurry, her head pounding. Colors were too bright. Sounds too loud. Everything amplified to nauseating proportions.

"They know we're ready. They'll be tracking my cell-phone signal to find us. That may take a little time."

"I don't think I have a little time left in me." Her legs gave out, and she was on the ground, Jonas leaning over her, his cool hand pressed to her cheek.

"You're burning up." He brushed strands of hair from her forehead, his hand settling there.

"Funny. I feel like I'm freezing." Her teeth chattered, and he frowned, opening his pack, his jaw set, morning light falling on a hard, handsome face.

High cheekbones. Pitch black hair that fell past his collar. Blue-green eyes. Full, firm lips. An ancient warrior come to life.

"You should have told me that you were feverish again."

"And slowed us down more than I already had? I don't think so."

"We lost our friends a couple hours ago. We could have stopped for a while." He handed her aspirin and water, glanced at his watch. His skin was deeply tan, his hands broad and strong. Climber's hands. Climber's forearms.

And Skylar shouldn't be noticing.

Wouldn't be noticing if she weren't out of her head with fever. After all, she'd tried the relationship thing, had dreamed of family and love, had pinned her hopes on a handsome, interesting man. All she'd gotten for her efforts was a broken heart.

She choked the aspirin down her swollen throat. Gagging, hoping it and the water wouldn't come right back up again.

"Take it easy."

"I don't think I have a choice." The world spun, and she closed her eyes, trying to still its whirling motion, feeling her heart fluttering, her pulse whooshing in her ears. A cold, wet cloth dropped onto her forehead, and she shivered, shoving it away, scowling when it ended up right back where it had been.

"Leave it, Grady. You're way too hot, and I don't plan on losing you when we're this close to safety." The tone was gruff, but she could hear the fear in it.

I watched my wife and unborn son die, and I was helpless to save them. The words whirled through her head, spinning with the world, mixing with Tessa's warning. *You stay too long in one place, and you'll die there.* And she wasn't sure who was sitting next to her. Wasn't sure if she was in the past or the present. Wasn't sure whose hand pressed the cold cloth to her head. Wasn't sure where she was, barely knew *who* she was.

"I'm not going to die, Tessa," she managed to say as cool fingers traced a path to the pulse point in her neck.

"You're too ornery to die." Jonas's voice came from far away, and she forced her eyes open.

"I'm not ornery." But she wasn't sure about the dying part. Her teeth chattered as Jonas tucked the Mylar blanket around her, eased up her head and slid his pack beneath it just as he'd done in the cave hours ago.

Was she still there? Still in the cave? The long climb, the long walk, the endless struggling, nothing more than a vivid dream?

She sat up, heart pounding too fast, the world spinning even faster. Tears spilling down her cheeks, and she didn't even know why.

"Shhhhhh." Jonas brushed moisture from her face, urged her back down. "You're fine, Grady."

"Am I dreaming?"

"You're sick."

"That much I knew."

He chuckled and shook his head as he pressed the cold cloth to her forehead again. She closed her eyes, wanting to escape the spinning world and the throbbing pain in her head, the burning pain in her throat. The lush desert landscape that had become her enemy.

"Tell me about Tessa." The words intruded on the velvety blackness Skylar was falling into, and she frowned.

"I'm too tired."

"Tell me anyway."

"You're trying to keep me awake, because you're afraid I'm going to die."

"Tell me about her."

"She was my older sister."

"Was?"

"Was. Is. I haven't seen her in fifteen years."

"You don't get along?"

"We did. She left home when she was sixteen."

"A runaway?"

"She would have been if there'd been anyone to report that she'd run, but my father was too steeped in alcohol to notice, and my mother overdosed a few years before Tessa left. There was no one but me, and I was too young to know what I should do. So, I just did what I'd been doing for years. I took care of Dad and went to school, took on more baby-sitting jobs and ran more errands for the neighbors to help with the bills." She was saying too much, telling Jonas things she'd never told anyone else. Not her good friends. Not any of the guys she'd dated. Not even Matthew, and they'd been months away from marriage before she'd realized what a slimeball he was.

"Who took care of you?"

"Like I said, I'm too tired for this." She closed her eyes, closed her mouth. Shut in all the things she could have said.

No one had taken care of her. For as long as she could remember, she'd taken care of herself. Made her own meals, washed her own clothes, cleaned her room and the house and mopped up puke and stale alcohol when her father went on a drinking binge. She'd learned to survive the hard way. Cut fingers from sharp knives. Blisters from hot pans, and reddened skin from scalding water. Cold nights when she forgot to pay the electric bill the year her mother died. By the time Tessa left, Skylar could run a house on her own.

She just hadn't wanted to.

Tears slid down her cheeks again.

Because she couldn't change the past. Couldn't save her mother or father or Tessa. Couldn't save Jonas's wife or his tiny baby. Couldn't even save herself.

Wings beat the air. Giant vultures swooping down to devour her before she was even dead, and Skylar gasped, opening her eyes to whirling wind and pounding chopper blades. Jonas stood a few feet away, waving at the pilot as the helicopter touched down.

She stood, swaying, wanting to run toward safety and civilization and everything she'd spent almost a week struggling for, but her feet were glued to the ground, her body too weak. She tried to call Jonas back, but her throat was hot and tight, what little sound she made swept away on the rushing wind.

He turned anyway. As if he'd heard her. Sensed her.

A foolish thought, but it stayed as he frowned, the irritation on his face overshadowed by the concern in his eyes.

"You just don't know when to stay down, do you?" He swept her into his arms, lifting her easily.

A knight in shining armor.

A warrior hero.

A *man*.

She'd learned her lesson about men just like she'd learned everything else in life—the hard way.

They couldn't be trusted. They couldn't be counted on.

The world spun as Jonas jogged to the helicopter, handed

her over the waiting medic. A sack of potatoes. That's what she felt like. A bruised and battered bag. Someone wrapped another blanket around her shoulders, asked her a question she couldn't hear or didn't understand. She didn't know which, couldn't think past the quick movement and twirling world, the rapid pulse of chopper blades and howling wind.

Jonas.

Where was he?

She searched for him as she was strapped to a backboard and lifted onto the chopper, and he was there, leaning close so that his lips brushed her ear. "I'm going to backtrack to the mesa, see if I can find our friends' trail. If I do, it'll give the police something to go on."

"No!" she shouted, loudly enough that the medic pressed a gentle hand to her shoulder.

"You need to relax, Ms. Grady. You've been through a lot."

"I'm not leaving without—"

But Jonas was already gone, slipping away before she could grab his hand and try to keep him from going.

She struggled against the straps that held her in place, and the medic leaned close, looked in her eyes. "Ma'am, you're going to have to calm down."

"You can't leave Jonas behind."

"It's his choice. Not ours. The sooner you settle down, the sooner we can get you to Phoenix and come back." The medic's tone was firm, but there was sympathy in his dark brown eyes.

"But—"

"Jonas Sampson is one tough son of a gun. He's traveled this area more than any other person I know. You don't have to worry about him. Just worry about yourself and getting healthy again. Now I'm going to hook you up to some fluids, try to get your fever down. You'll feel better about everything when you're not burning up." He swabbed the inside of her elbow with alcohol, told her to hold still.

She didn't feel the pinch as the line was placed, felt nothing but numb dismay and scorching heat and the awful knowledge that she'd made it out of the desert, but that she'd left Jonas behind.

Keep him safe, Lord. Please.

The chopper lifted off, and Skylar's world shifted, tilted, sideways and back and up and down, and she spun into a vortex of images and sounds. Desert and rain and caves and climbs. Guns and shadows. Tessa reaching for her, and Skylar reaching back. Light and darkness, and finally nothing, but silence. The velvety darkness she'd longed for seeping in, covering it all.

Except for him.

The knight.

The hero.

The man.

Jonas, his words whispering in her ear.

I was helpless to save either of them. I'm not helpless to save you.

He'd proven his words.

He'd saved her.

But could he save himself?

SEVEN

Jonas hated hospitals.

Hated the scent and sound and feel of them.

The frantic energy that poured from the people that moved through the emergency room ebbed and flowed like the tide, tugging Jonas with it.

If he let himself, he could fall into an emotional time warp, feel what he'd felt the night Gabriella was shot. See everything—his blood-soaked dress shoes, his stained-red hands hanging limply between his knees as he waited for news he knew would not be good.

She'd been dead before the ambulance arrived at the scene. Probably dead before he'd pressed frantic hands over the blood spurting from her chest.

A bullet straight to the heart.

No way to save her.

Nothing that could have been done.

Those had been the doctor's words, but Jonas had only heard his own recriminations.

He'd moved Gabriella from Phoenix to New Mexico to pursue his dream of becoming a border patrol agent. In the end, his dream had killed her and their son. Time had healed some of his sorrow, but it hadn't assuaged his guilt.

He felt it acutely as he strode through the waiting room and approached the receptionist. "Excuse me—"

"Go ahead and sign in. We'll call you back in a few minutes," she said without looking up, and he bit back impatience. It wasn't her fault he'd been waylaid by the police as soon as he'd gotten off the helicopter. Not her fault he'd spent the past hour and a half explaining what had happened out in the desert.

Not her fault that he was hungry, tired and ready to be done with the hospital.

No one's fault but his own that he'd allowed Kane to talk him into searching for Skylar.

Talk him into it?

Kane had asked. Jonas had said yes. Simple as that.

He'd gotten the call three days ago, and, for the first time in years, Jonas had felt a buzz of excitement, a hum of adrenaline. He'd gone with it. Reported to search and rescue, asked to be allowed access to the site where Skylar's jeep had been found. Not expecting that he'd find a woman alive, but expecting that he could at least help a friend in need find closure.

He *had* found Skylar alive, though, and he planned to make sure she stayed that way.

"I'm hoping you can help me find a patient that arrived by chopper a couple hours ago. Skylar Grady." He kept his voice even and his expression pleasant, and the receptionist finally looked up.

"You mean the woman who was missing in the desert for a week?"

"That's the one."

"She's been admitted. Are you a friend or family member?"

"I'm Jonas Sampson. I—"

"You found her. I guess that makes you a friend. She's

already been admitted." She typed something into the computer, read the information that popped up on the screen. "Room 432. Visitation is limited, so check in at the nurse's station before you go in."

"Thanks." He hurried through the emergency room, pulling out his cell phone as he went. He needed to call Kane, let him know Skylar had been found.

"Dougherty here. You have news?"

"You were right. Skylar is too stubborn to die."

"You found her?" The relief in Kane's voice was unmistakable, and that feeling Jonas had, the one that said he was doing what he was meant to be doing, using his skill the way he was meant to, settled deep, surprising him. He hadn't had that in a long time. He'd forgotten how good it felt. An instant later, he pushed the feeling away. This wasn't his life anymore. This was just a favor to a friend. He couldn't let it be anything more.

He'd found Skylar and now he was going to make arrangements for her to fly back to New York, just like he'd promised in the first place. Then, all of this would be over.

Yeah, right. As if it would really be that easy.

"We're at Phoenix General Hospital."

"Is she okay?"

"She should be. I'm heading up to her room now. I was held up by the police and haven't seen her since she arrived."

"Police?"

"We've got a problem, Kane. A big one. Whatever you sent Skylar here to do, she's in it deep. Deep enough that someone wants her dead." He filled in Kane on what little he knew, explained what had happened in the desert.

"I sent her to find a guy who owes back child support. That shouldn't be enough to bring out a posse. I want her on the next plane back to New York. Tell her I'll send a couple people out to track down Redmond and figure out what's going on."

"I'll tell her." But he doubted she'd listen. Sick as she'd been, she'd climbed a hundred and fifty feet straight up, walked all night, and managed to fight Jonas most of the way while she was doing it. She wasn't going to turn tail and run because Kane said she should.

"She's going to refuse, so you're going to have to find a way to convince her." Kane said exactly what Jonas was thinking.

"Me? You're her boss. It seems like you should be the one to convince her."

"And it seems to *me* that you've run short on backbone."

"What's that supposed to mean?"

"That if I didn't know better, I'd think you were afraid to face down a 120-pound woman."

"Nice try, Kane, but we're not college students anymore. You can't convince me to do something by calling me chicken." He punched the elevator button, anxious to get up to Skylar's room, make sure she was okay.

Make sure she was there.

Based on what he'd seen out in the desert, he wouldn't be surprised if she was planning an escape.

"I figured as much, but I had to try. The truth is, there's no way Skylar is going to listen to me."

"But you think she'll listen to me?"

"You saved her life. That has to have some value." Jonas got on the elevator, wished things would be as easy as Kane was making them sound.

Go up to the room.

Convince Skylar to leave town.

Go back to his life.

"Guilt value, you mean?"

"Whatever works."

"I don't have to tell you that nothing will work, do I?"

"I'd appreciate the effort, anyway. If you can't get her on the plane…I hate to ask, but—"

"I'll keep an eye on her. Do what I can to help with the investigation."

"I can pay you an hourly wage. Same rate I pay my part-time investigators. Just submit a bill once she's back home."

"No. And don't insult me by offering again. I'll keep you posted." He disconnected before Kane could argue. They'd been friends since college, had supported each other through some tough times. He'd help because of that, and because he wasn't going to walk away and leave Skylar to fight her battle alone.

A nurse looked up as he stepped off the elevator, offering a quizzical smile. "Can I help you?"

"I'm here to visit Skylar Grady."

"I'm sorry. That won't be possible. She can't have visitors, yet. Maybe, tomorrow—"

"It's going to have to be today. I just spent fifteen hours getting her out of the desert, and I want to make sure she's okay."

"Oh." Her eyes widened, and she smiled. "You're the Shadow Wolf who finally managed to track her down."

"I was a Shadow Wolf, ma'am. Now I'm a contractor." Apparently news was traveling fast. He'd known when he'd handed Skylar to Tanner Morgan that it would. They'd been buddies in high school, had lost touch for a few years and reconnected when Jonas moved back to Arizona.

"Sorry." She blushed. "Ms. Grady's room is just down the hall to the left."

"Thanks." He strode down the corridor, nearly walking into Skylar as she stepped out of her room.

"Jonas! What are you doing here?"

"Coming to see you. Seems like I was almost too late."

"Actually, you're just in time. I need a ride back to Cave Creek."

"You don't really think I'm going to give you one, do you?" She was hooked up to an IV, and he slid the pole from her grasp, gently urging her back into the room.

"I was hoping." She collapsed onto the bed, bare feet and legs sticking out from under a cotton hospital gown. Knicks and scratches covered both shins, and her feet were blistered and raw. Someone had braided her hair, pulling the wild mane of curls back to reveal sunburned cheeks and a bruised forehead.

"Tell you what, I'll give you a ride to the airport. Get you on a plane to New York." He grabbed a chair, settled into it.

"You don't really think I'm going to let you do that, do you?" She threw back at him, closely mimicking his response to her request.

"I'd probably be disappointed if you did. Or think you were a lot sicker than you look."

"I look like a train wreck, and this isn't doing anything to improve things." She plucked at the neck of her hospital gown, her fingers brushing the arrowhead he'd given her.

"I see you still have this." He touched the cool stone, then her cheek, feeling for a fever. Warm. Not hot. Smooth and silky despite the sunburn and scratches. He had the urge to linger there, let his fingers explore the sharp angle of her cheekbone, the gentle curve of her jaw. Surprised, he dropped his hand away.

"They tried to take it from me in the emergency room, but I told the nurse if she reached for it again, I'd take her arm off."

"Nice."

"I wasn't in the best frame of mind. What with you ditching me and heading back into the desert alone and all. I figured if you died, your family might want this, and I didn't want the hospital to lose it. Since you're here—" She started to drag it over her head, but he stopped her.

"Do you always try to return gifts?"

"It wasn't a gift. It was an award. Something given in jest."

"I don't give anything in jest, Grady."

"Then, thank you. It's beautiful. I couldn't see it last night, but your grandfather was quite an artisan." She let the arrowhead fall, her fingers twirling one of the turquoise beads Pops had crafted and strung on the leather cord.

"You were on your way out of the room when I got here. Where were you headed?"

"To the nurse's station. I want this IV out."

"You need the fluids."

"So the doctor told me. Over and over and *over* again. Fluids and an antibiotic. I told him to give me a couple bottles of water and a prescription, but he refused." She frowned, standing up and pacing across the room, dragging the IV pole behind her.

"You've been through—"

"Jonas, if you tell me that I've been through a lot and say I need to rest, I will take this IV pole and knock you over the head with it." She scowled, her dark eyes flashing with irritation.

"Feeling a little ornery, Grady?"

She shot him a heated look, then shook her head, offering a sheepish grin. "Maybe. Every nurse and doctor who's looked at me has said the same thing. *You've been through a lot. You need to rest.* The thing is, I've been through worse than a six-day hike. I know my body, and it's saying that another round of antibiotics and a good meal will do me a lot more good than a hospital room and an IV. Besides, sticking around makes me feel like a sitting duck. Anyone could walk in here. I don't have a weapon since the doctor insisted on passing the one we confiscated on to the police. I'm not sure I have the strength to hold my own in a physical fight."

"So, you want to go to ground for a while, hide out until you're feeling better?"

She hesitated, fingered the arrowhead again. "You could say that."

"*I* could, but *you're* not?"

"I want a safe place to crash for a few hours, but I want justice more. Unless you managed to round up the entire posse of bad guys when you went back into the desert, I've got some work to do before I get that rest."

"I'm afraid I came up empty. I found a trail that the police are following, but that's it."

"Like I said, I have work to do." She walked toward the door again, and he grabbed her arm, pulled her to a stop.

"This isn't a good idea, Grady."

"And staying here is? We don't know who was out in the desert with us, Jonas. Until we do, I don't trust anyone. Not doctors, not nurses, not people wandering through the halls. This place is teeming with all three."

"It's a hospital. What else did you expect?"

"Look, maybe I sound paranoid and maybe leaving *isn't* the best idea, but the last time I didn't listen to my instincts, I got shot three times and came so close to dying the doctors still don't know how I lived. Right now my instincts are telling me to get out of here. That's what I plan to do. You can help me or not. Either way, as soon as I get this IV taken out, I'm hitting the road."

"You know what would make me happy, Grady?" he muttered, and she met his gaze, her dark eyes flashing.

"The better question is, 'Do I care?'"

"Of course you do. I'm the one who dragged you out of the desert, after all."

"I can't believe you're playing the guilt card." She scowled, and he smiled.

"Kane's suggestion. Is it working?"

"No."

"Too bad, because the thing that would make me happy is if your instincts were telling you to hop on the next plane out of town."

"Sorry to disappoint you. I'm staying in Arizona until I get the answers I want."

She would, too. He knew it, didn't know why he'd even bothered arguing. "In that case, you've got yourself a bodyguard. Stay put. I'll get a nurse to take out the IV."

"Bodyguard? What are you talking about?" she sputtered, but he ignored the question and walked out into the corridor. As much as he hated to admit it, Skylar had a point. They didn't know who'd been out in the desert with them, couldn't know who her enemies were or where they might show up. Getting her out of the hospital and into a secure location wasn't such a bad idea.

And he knew exactly where that location would be.

An hour later, he'd managed to talk the doctor into writing a prescription for Skylar's antibiotics, convince the police to run a patrol by his place, boot his sister out of the garage apartment for a few nights and arrange for his father and stepmother to drop off his truck at the hospital.

He shoved his cell phone into his pocket, watching while the nurse took out Skylar's IV and pressed a Band-Aid into place. "You're all set, Ms. Grady. Your clothes are in the drawer, and the doctor's instructions are here." She handed Skylar a sheet of paper.

"Thanks."

"You'll need to follow up with your personal physician in the next day or two, and if you have any questions or concerns, please don't hesitate to contact Dr. Sawyer. Here is the prescription the pharmacy filled for you. Now just hold tight while I get the wheelchair."

She hurried away, and Skylar dug out her clothes from the drawer. "Six days didn't treat these very well."

"Here." Jonas pulled clean jeans and a T-shirt from his backpack. "They'll be big, but they might be a better option."

"Almost anything would be better. Thanks." She smiled, and his breath caught in surprise at the beauty of it. He turned away, uncomfortable with his reaction. In the past year, friends had tried setting him up with sisters, cousins and friends of friends. He'd gone out a few times, had pleasant dates with pleasant women who'd left him feeling nothing but mild interest. Gabriella had been his first and only real love. Four years after her death, and he knew he'd never find another woman like her. Wasn't really interested in trying to.

Skylar was nothing like her. So what was it about the woman that had him so intrigued?

Nothing, that's what.

He wasn't intrigued, he was annoyed, exhausted and ready to say goodbye to Skylar and her problems.

Ready, but not able.

Even if he hadn't agreed to keep an eye on her, he couldn't walk away. Not when he knew how much danger she was in.

She might not want a bodyguard, but she was getting one.

It was as simple as that.

He walked out into the hall, waiting impatiently while Skylar changed, his thoughts jumping ahead, plotting their next step the way he had when he'd worked border patrol.

He and Skylar had been at a disadvantage the previous night, outnumbered and outgunned, taken by surprise. Here, things were different. The perps' approach would have to be different, too. They'd have to come one at a time or risk being detected before they attacked. But the advantage wouldn't truly be on his and Skylar's side until they figured out who was after her. And why.

"They're a little big, but I'm making them work." Skylar stepped into the corridor.

"A little big" was an understatement.

Faded jeans brushed the floor, despite the number of times she'd rolled the cuffs. His worn blue shirt hung almost to her knees, the crew neck slipping to reveal hints of creamy skin and a scar that ran down the middle of her sternum.

She must have noticed the direction of his gaze, because she hiked the shirt back into place, covered the scar with her hand.

"There's no need to try to hide it," he said.

"There is if I want to avoid questions." She let her hand fall away, offered a smile that didn't reach her eyes.

"Too late for that."

"I figured as much."

"Is that from one of the bullets?"

"Yes."

"What happened?"

"A dirty partner. A drug bust that went bad. Movie-of-the-week stuff. Or maybe soap opera. I still haven't figured out which."

"What happened to your partner?"

"He was killed during the gunfight. Friendly fire. At least, that's what everyone said until I was able to tell them he wasn't a friend. This—" she gestured to the scar "—was his work. He shot me almost before I'd realized he'd pulled a gun." She touched the edge of the scar, then tugged the shirt into place to cover the purple ridge.

"I'm sorry."

"Don't be. I'm alive, and I've learned from the experience." She limped to the empty nurse's station, her wet shoes squeaking with every step. "Looks like the nurse is still searching for a wheelchair. We may as well go." She punched the elevator button.

"There's no hurry. Our ride isn't here yet, and I don't want to stand outside waiting for it. No sense giving a sniper the chance to take a shot."

"I'm not planning to give anyone a chance to do anything. I need to sit down somewhere quiet, think things through. Try to figure out why searching for a guy like Daniel Redmond would put me on someone's hit list."

"That's the guy you were hunting?"

"Yes." The elevator doors opened, and she stepped in, turning to face him. Her eyes were chocolate brown, her lashes thick and black. Even without makeup, even with her skin red and raw, even drowning in Jonas's old clothes, she was striking. Average height. Average weight. But there was absolutely nothing average about her.

The thought surprised him as much as his visceral reaction to her smile had.

"Did anyone in Cave Creek have any idea of his whereabouts?"

"No one who would admit it. Someone knows, though. Someone who either told Redmond I was closing in, leading him to attack me, or who doesn't want me to find him." She leaned against the wall, her face pallid, her eyes deeply shadowed.

"Either that or the people who are after you have nothing to do with Redmond." He pressed a hand to her lower back, urging her into the lobby.

"There's no other option, Jonas."

"Seems like a private investigator would have plenty of other options."

"True, but my most recent cases have involved tracking runaways or finding estranged family members. Nothing that would put me on someone's hit list. Even if I did manage to annoy someone enough to become a target, it would have been easier and cheaper to kill me off in New York. Why follow me here?"

"To put the police off the trail?"

"I'd say that was a reasonable assumption if there hadn't been a dozen or so people chasing after me last night. I don't have any clients with big money. None of the people I've tracked are rich. It takes plenty of resources to hire a small army."

"You've got a point." He led her to a chair, planning to insist she sit, but the double entrance doors opened, and two people walked into the lobby.

Two very familiar people.

Jonas braced for the onslaught as one broke away from the other, racing toward him as fast as her high-heeled feet would allow.

EIGHT

"Jonas! Thank goodness you're all right. We've been worried sick." A short, plump blonde raced across the lobby and straight into Jonas's arms. She offered him a tight hug, then turned to Skylar. A few years past fifty, the corners of her eyes lined from years of smiling, she had the kind of effortless, natural beauty that would last far into the next decades of life.

Jonas's mother? Before she could decide, the woman grabbed her hand, patted her knuckles. "You poor thing. You've been through a horrible experience. We need to get you home and tucked into bed."

"I—" Skylar tried to protest, but the woman wrapped an arm around her waist and led her toward the exit. It felt odd, the closeness. Shoulder to shoulder. Arm to arm. As if they were family rather than strangers.

"Debby, if you keep smothering the girl, she won't make it to the car, much less to Jonas's place," a tall lanky man said. Closing in on sixty, his hair more gray than brown, he had the same blue-green eyes as Jonas.

"I'm not smothering. I'm supporting."

"In case you haven't figured it out, these are my father Richard and his wife, Debby." Jonas offered a wry smile, hanging back as if he felt as uncomfortable as Skylar.

Maybe he did.

Families weren't always what they should be. Skylar knew that as well as anyone. Maybe Jonas's relationship with Debby and Richard was as strained as Skylar's had once been with her family. Love mixed with fear and disappointment and anger.

"It's nice to meet you both." Her voice still sounded as raw and sore as her throat felt, and Debby patted her arm.

"I've got some of my homemade chicken noodle soup already at the apartment where you'll be staying. You'll have to have some of it tonight. It will do wonders for you."

"You shouldn't have gone to the trouble."

"It's no trouble. I love cooking. As a matter of fact, it's my life's work."

"Debby has a catering business," Jonas explained as he said goodbye to his dad and Debby, his hand on Skylar's shoulder as they walked outside. Late afternoon sunlight streamed onto the sidewalk, splashing patterns and shadows onto the ground. The contrast made Skylar's head spin, and she swayed, reaching out, grabbing Jonas's arm.

"You okay?"

"Right as rain." Except that her head was still spinning, her stomach churning.

"Then why do you look pale as paper?" He helped her into the passenger seat of a beat-up Chevy truck, reached across her lap to snap the seat belt into place.

"Maybe my sunburn is wearing off."

He chuckled, the rough sound washing over her as she leaned back, closed her eyes. Quiet voices drifted into the truck, but she didn't look to see who was speaking. Didn't want to chance being overtaken by dizziness again. Passing out in front of the hospital would mean going right back where she didn't want to be. Vulnerable. Alone. But she wasn't alone. Jonas was with her—along with his family.

And if danger followed her, she could be bringing it to his home. She shivered.

"Cold?" Jonas tucked something around her shoulders, his callused hands more familiar, more welcome than she wanted them to be.

"Worrying that I'm putting your family at risk. I don't want anything to happen to them."

"Neither do I. I told them they should keep their distance until we figure things out."

"I hope their feelings weren't hurt."

"I'd rather have their feelings hurt than endanger their lives."

"I feel the same. Which is why I know your feelings won't be hurt when I tell you I want you to bring me to the closest Phoenix police station and drop me off."

He didn't respond, and she opened her eyes. "Well?"

"What?"

"I asked you to drop me off at the police station."

"I would have responded, but I figured that either your fever is back and you're delusional, or you didn't hear me the half dozen times that I told you I'm sticking around until you are on your way back to New York." He pulled onto a long stretch of highway, his jaw tight with irritation.

"I can't ask you to—"

"You didn't ask."

"Jonas—"

"Tell you what, we'll work together, try to figure out what's going on. If things get too hot, you'll get on a plane and leave town, and I'll go back to my life."

"That doesn't work for me."

"It's going to have to."

"You're exasperating."

"Thanks, I've always thought it went well with rude."

The comment surprised a laugh out of her, and she gave

up the fight. Jonas wasn't backing down and, truth be told, Skylar was glad. She'd been alone for six days. It felt good to have someone around.

Six days?

She'd been alone for fifteen *years*.

Unless she counted the two years she'd wasted dating Matthew. She preferred not to.

"You're quiet."

"My throat is protesting. I'm trying to give it a break." It was a partial truth, and she was sure Jonas knew it.

He met her eyes, the contact brief, but so filled with questions Skylar turned away, stared out at the passing landscape. He already knew too much. Had already seen her vulnerable and scared and out of her head with fever. Seen more than anyone ever had.

"You have your prescription?"

She nodded, patting her pocket and the plastic bottle of medicine there. She didn't speak, though. Just rested her head on the window, the rhythm of the truck matching the pulsing rhythm of her heart. She let it carry her away from the pain, the truck, Jonas and his unspoken questions. Let herself drift for just a little while.

"Skylar?" A callused hand smoothed hair from her cheek, and she jerked upright, scared out of her mind that she was back where she'd been a week ago, lying on the front seat of the jeep, the sun streaming in through the window, scorching her face.

"Where are we?" She looked into ocean blue eyes, fear slipping away as reality took hold. The hospital visit. The truck ride. *Jonas.*

"My place." Jonas got out of the truck, and she did the same, stumbling from the cab with little grace, her movements shaky and disjointed.

To her left, a small house stood in the middle of a landscaped yard. Yellow stucco bungalow. Whitewashed front porch. Baskets of flowers hanging from the eaves. Comfortable, homey. Nothing like the house she'd imagined Jonas living in. Everything like the one she'd once dreamed would be hers.

She'd wanted it so much. The pretty little house. The kids laughing in the yard. The family she could go home to.

"It's adorable."

"Thanks. I think."

"Adorable is good."

"I'd prefer masculine and tough, but my sister's vision is a lot different than mine, and I gave her carte blanche when she moved into the garage apartment." He gestured to a detached garage that sat a few yards from the house, an external stairway leading up to a second-story door.

"She's a decorator?"

"A social worker. At least, she will be once she finishes her master's thesis. She has a good eye, though, just like Debby, and she knows how to make a house a home. It made sense to let her take charge of the cosmetics."

"Jonas!" The apartment door flew open, and a curvy blonde hurried down the stairs. Mid-twenties, Skylar estimated, her hair falling in a sleek bob to her chin, she looked as effortlessly beautiful as Debby.

"I thought you were going to clear out before we got here," Jonas growled, and the young woman shrugged.

"I'm packing."

"For a few days, Rayne, not a year. That doesn't take an hour and a half."

"It does when a person actually cares about how she looks." She patted her hair, offering a saucy smile that made her seem even younger than Skylar had first thought. "Besides, I wanted to meet your guest. I'm Rayne Sampson." She offered a hand, and Skylar took it.

"Skylar Grady."

"I know. My mother filled me in. Said I should take out a container of her chicken-noodle soup and let it thaw, because you'd need it. I think you need a change of clothes and a shower more. Am I right? Come on. I'll show you around, get you settled before I head out." She slid an arm around Skylar's waist, the same way her mother had done at the hospital.

"You're staying with Debby and Dad, right?" Jonas followed them up the stairs and into a small living room, his presence dwarfing the comfortable couch and easy chair, overshadowing the homey decorations. He'd been larger than life out in the desert. The small room only showcased his height, the breadth of his shoulders, the force of his gaze.

"Tonight, I'm staying with Rachel. We were planning on heading to the college library to work, then getting some dinner, so it made more sense than driving all the way from the university to Mom and Dad's place."

"You didn't tell Rachel why you needed a place to stay, did you?"

"I may be your younger sister, Jonas, but I'm not a child. I've seen the news. I know some crazy things are going on, and I figured you are trying to keep Skylar hidden away for a few days. If anyone finds out she's here, it won't be because of me."

"Sorry. It's been a long few days." Jonas raked a hand over glossy black hair, and Skylar couldn't help thinking that no one should look so good after tromping through the desert and running for his life. He met her eyes, and she realized she'd been staring. Realized she'd been thinking things she shouldn't. Things about the way he looked, the way she felt when his ocean-blue eyes settled on her. Shaky and unsure and intrigued.

She knew the feelings.

Knew what they meant.

Didn't like it.

Because those feelings were exactly what had gotten her into trouble with Matthew. Handsome, charming, *lying* Matthew.

"I pulled out a couple things for you. A shirt, some jeans. They're on the bed in my room. There's a washing machine in here. Feel free to wash anything you need to." Rayne pulled open a small closet, and Skylar nodded, thankful for the distraction.

"I appreciate you giving up your apartment, Rayne."

"It's no problem. I'm barely here anymore anyway. Between my work and my school, there isn't a lot of time to chill." She smiled, light spilling in from the bay window and highlighting hollows beneath her cheekbones and circles under her eyes. Covered by a deft hand and sheer makeup, they disappeared as Rayne stepped into a galley kitchen. "The soup is in the fridge. Mom suggests you pour it into a saucepan. Me? I'd microwave it."

"How about we skip the instructions, you grab your bag and get out of here, sis?" Jonas broke in, and Rayne frowned.

"What's the hurry?"

"You said it yourself. There's some crazy stuff going on. I don't want you caught up in any of it."

"I deal with crazy stuff every day at the shelter. What's the difference?" But she grabbed a laptop, shoved it into a case along with a file folder overflowing with paper.

"The difference is, this is *my* crazy stuff. Come on." He lifted an overnight case that sat near the door, pulled the laptop from his sister's hands.

"My brother is bossy, in case you haven't noticed." Rayne opened a kitchen drawer and grabbed a handful of chocolate bars, apparently not at all concerned by Jonas's hard glare.

"I have," Skylar responded, liking Rayne more with every passing moment.

"I'm standing right here, ladies." And he was getting impatient, pent-up energy rolling off him and filling the small room..

"And standing there for another minute isn't going to kill you," Rayne shot back as she slung a purse over her shoulder.

"It's not *me* being killed that I'm worried about," he growled, and Rayne handed Skylar one of the candy bars.

"One of my not-so-secret stashes. Help yourself to more if you feel the need. Since you're hanging out with Jonas, you probably will." She laughed when Jonas shoved open the door, stepped onto the small stoop at the top of the stairs and gestured for her to follow.

"Guess that's my cue to hit the road. It was really nice meeting you, Skylar."

"You, too."

Rayne smiled, her deep blue eyes looking straight into Skylar's. Probing, seeking, the intensity exactly like Jonas's before she pulled Skylar in for a hug.

"Be careful, okay? My brother's heart was broken once. I'd hate for it to happen again." The words were barely a whisper. Before Skylar could register their meaning, Rayne stepped back, offered an easy smile and walked outside.

"Go ahead and get settled. I'll be back up later." Jonas issued the command and closed the door, shutting Skylar into the cozy apartment.

Alone.

Again.

She frowned, irritated with her need for company. She'd spent her entire adult life living alone. She'd never needed anyone. Not even Matthew. She'd *wanted* him. Or, at least, wanted what he represented, but he'd filled none of the emptiness in Skylar's heart, plugged none of the holes that had been left by her family.

Maybe that should have been the first clue that he wasn't the guy for her. That there was probably no guy for her.

For her, love and family were elusive dreams. The harder she'd tried to hold onto them, the more quickly they slipped away. After Matthew, she'd given up trying. She had her life, her faith. She had friends. She had her work that made her feel like she was making a difference. She didn't need a husband or kids to fulfill her.

But she *had* wanted them.

Wanted all the things she'd been denied when she was a skinny little girl living in squalor.

"Stop it," she hissed, shoving aside the melancholy mood and the memories and grabbing the clothes and boots Rayne had left out for her.

She showered and changed, pulling on jeans that were a size too big and a cowl-necked sweater that showed too much of her scar. She tossed her sneakers into the trash, made a circuit of the apartment, even tested out the bed, but she was too restless to sleep. Too pent up to close her eyes. Despite her sore throat and throbbing headache, despite her fatigue, she needed to work. Needed to find answers. Find Redmond.

And then she needed to get back to New York and move on with her life. Exactly as she'd planned she would.

No more regrets. No more secret longings. No more feeling as if life were passing her by.

No more gazing into blue-green eyes and feeling her heart flutter.

She scowled.

Her heart did *not* flutter when she looked into Jonas's eyes.

Much.

She dropped down in front of a small desk in the corner

of the living room, booted up the computer. She'd log into her email account, print out some of the notes she'd sent to Kane. She'd missed something when she was questioning the residents of Cave Creek. Something big enough to nearly get her killed. Maybe reading through the notes would clarify things.

She tore open the chocolate bar, bit into it. She felt light-headed and worn, but she needed to keep going, needed to find answers quickly. Her life depended on it.

And, if the way she felt when she looked into Jonas's eyes was any indication, her heart might, too.

NINE

An hour seemed like more than enough time for Skylar to get settled into the apartment.

More than enough time for her to get into trouble, too.

Jonas crossed the yard that separated the house from the garage, jogged up the stairs and knocked on the door.

Nothing. No voice calling for him to come in.

Or to go away.

No movement. Not even a hint that Skylar was inside.

He knocked again, waited a heartbeat and opened the door.

Silence greeted him, and he surveyed the room, saw Skylar at the desk, cheek pressed to the wood, damp curls spilling down her back. A half-eaten candy bar lay near her hand, and a pile of papers sat near the printer. She didn't move as he walked toward her, barely seemed to be breathing.

Out cold.

Completely oblivious.

She seemed more vulnerable than when he'd found her in the desert, more fragile than she'd appeared in the hospital.

"Sky?" He touched her cheek, wasn't surprised when she didn't respond. Even the toughest person couldn't keep pushing forever. Skylar had reached her limit hours ago.

He lifted her from the chair, her solid weight reminding him of long ago days. Gabriella laughing up into his eyes as he carried her across the threshold of their New Mexico home, whispering sweet promises into his ear as he twirled her around the day she'd found out she was pregnant. The memories were bittersweet, and he swallowed them back as he settled Skylar onto the bed, pulled an afghan over her.

Nothing like Gabriella.

The thought flitted through his mind, just as it had at the hospital.

Gabriella had been bright and sunny and sweet. No darkness in her eyes. No shadows. Joy and faith and trust, they were as natural to her as they were foreign to Jonas, and he hadn't been able to resist their pull. Hers.

A moth to a flame, that's how he'd been, and he'd thrown himself into marriage the same way he'd thrown himself into everything. Eagerly.

It should have lasted longer.

Should have been the forever they'd both planned.

He turned, the movement sharp and rigid with all that he felt, and was surprised when Skylar grabbed his hand.

"Are you leaving?" Her eyes were glassy, her words slurred. More asleep than awake.

"Just heading over to my place to shower and change. I'm going to set the alarm. If anyone tries to get in, it'll go off here and at the house. Don't try to be a hero. Lock the bedroom door and stay put. Let me handle any intruders."

"A hero? There aren't many of those in this world, Jonas. I'm not one of them, but I'm beginning to think you may be."

"I'm no hero."

"No? Then how could you possibly be mine?"

"Go back to sleep, Skylar." His voice was gruffer than he'd intended, but Skylar didn't hear. She was already out again, dark lashes fanned across pink cheeks, her breath coming even and slow. His stomach clenched, his pulse leaping with thoughts he had no business entertaining.

Nothing like Gabriella, but Skylar was a flame in her own right, the shadows in her eyes, the secrets hidden there, calling out to Jonas in the same way Gabriella's openness had.

The thought followed him as he set the alarm and returned to his house, a cobweb he couldn't brush off no matter how much he tried.

He showered quickly, grabbed a cheese stick from the fridge, paced across the kitchen floor.

The silence of the house, the emptiness of it, mocked him, reminding him of the plans he and Gabriella had made, the dreams they'd shared.

He rubbed the back of his neck and scowled.

Obviously, the past few days had taken a toll on him. He was thinking too much about the past, letting his mind dwell where it shouldn't.

He'd moved on, but he hadn't let go.

Rayne had told him that a dozen times in the past few months, urging him to date again, to think about the future, to find God's plan for his life.

Not restoring old homes, either, bro. You're good at it, but you're better at what you were doing before. Finding people. It's a God-given gift. How long are you going to keep wasting it?

How much of a gift could it be when it cost him the ones he loved the most? What kind of hero couldn't save his own wife and child? *How could you possibly be mine,* Skylar had said. As if he *were* her hero. Could he handle that responsibility?

He'd lost his way since the murders, let himself drift along on the path of least resistance. Forgotten who he was, and maybe even who he was meant to be.

God's plan.

God who'd let Gabriella's life slip away, let baby Simon die before ever taking his first breath. God who hadn't intervened to save either of them.

Jonas lifted a photo from the coffee table. Gabriella as she'd been three weeks before the murder. Glowing with health, her belly pressing against the button-down shirt she'd borrowed from his closet, her hands resting on her stomach.

We are so blessed, Jonas. God is so good to us.

He could remember the moment like it was yesterday.

If he had been the one murdered, if she had lost their son and Jonas in one day, in one heartbeat, she would have accepted the tragedy for what it was and laid the blame where it belonged, on the evil that dwelled in the world rather than on God. But he didn't know if he could do that, even now.

The phone rang, and he grabbed it, eager for a distraction. "Sampson here."

"Sampson, this is Rodger Smithson, sheriff of Cave Creek. Sergeant Maria Jessop with the Phoenix P.D. gave me your number. I'm trying to reach Skylar Grady."

"She's resting."

"We were relieved to hear that she'd been found alive, and I wanted to thank you for your part in that."

"There was an entire search-and-rescue team involved."

"But you were the only one able to track her. Everyone around here will sleep better tonight. We were looking out for her while she was here, and it didn't feel right knowing she'd gone missing from our town. She's doing well, then?"

"As well as can be expected."

"Good. Good. I have her things down here at the station. Suitcase. Laptop. Everything that was in the hotel room. Plus, a few things we pulled from the jeep. Wish we'd treated them like evidence when we found them but, at the time, there was no reason to think there'd been foul play. She's free to come get the stuff when she's ready."

"I'll let her know."

"Great. We'd also like to take statements from both of you. We'll be working closely with Phoenix P.D., but since Skylar was abducted in our town, the investigation is in our jurisdiction. The sooner you two can get in for that, the better."

"Like I said, Skylar is sleeping."

"You could wake her."

"I could."

"But you won't?"

"No."

"The thing is, Sampson, it's imperative that we get this investigation moving. The longer it takes for us to have access to Skylar, the less likely it will be that we'll find the person responsible."

"Persons."

"Pardon?"

"There were at least ten people on the desert last night. You might want to send some men out. See what they can find. I gave the Phoenix police rough coordinates for some markers I left. A bloodhound might be able to pick up a scent and follow the trail."

"We could bring you out with us. I hear you're one of the best."

"Sorry, Sheriff, my days of tracking are over."

"You tracked Skylar."

"As a favor to a friend of mine and Skylar's."

"She's fortunate in her friends, then. Without you, she'd probably be dead."

"She was in Cave Creek searching for a man named Daniel Redmond." He ignored the sheriff's comment, the image of Skylar's blood seeping into rocky sand not one he wanted to dwell on.

"That's right."

"Did you know the man?"

"I knew of him. He worked at a diner around the corner from my office. Can't say we ever had much of a conversation, but he was new in town, so I kept my eye on him."

"Then you know who he hung out with? Who his friends were?"

There was a moment of silence, a hiss of breath. "Look, how about you just get Skylar and come in for a chat? We can discuss everything then."

"Is there a reason why you don't want to discuss it now?"

"I'd be happy to discuss it if I hadn't already covered all this with Skylar. The woman is like a pit bull. She gets hold of something, and she won't let it go."

"A good quality in an investigator."

"A good quality if it doesn't get a person killed. Listen, I have another phone call coming in. Come to the station with Skylar when you can. Like I said, the sooner the better." He hung up, and Jonas dropped the phone back into the receiver.

Skylar had said no one knew Redmond's whereabouts, but the sheriff had said he'd kept an eye on the guy. Surely, he knew the man's connections in town, his routines and habits.

Or maybe the claim was just that. Maybe the sheriff hadn't paid much attention to Redmond and was beating himself up over letting a deadbeat dad work in his town.

A high-pitched shriek filled the room, and Jonas's heart leaped, adrenaline coursing though him as the alarm pulsed its warning over and over again.

He pulled his gun, raced out the door, barreled into Skylar. "What are you doing out here? I told you to lock yourself in the room if the alarm went off." He dragged her in the house, pressing her against the wall, expecting bullets to fly.

"I set it off," she shouted, pushing against his arm, and putting her hands over her ears.

"What?" He typed in the alarm code, his ears ringing as the room fell silent.

"I said, I set off the alarm. I walked out the front door and it went off."

His jaw clenched, a million words he had no right to say dancing on the tip of his tongue.

Skylar was an adult, a former cop, a private investigator. She knew how to protect herself, knew how to be smart and how to survive, but he wanted to chew her out anyway. Tell her that she'd been a fool to walk outside when she knew a posse was gunning for her.

"Count to ten, Jonas, 'cause you look like you're about to blow." She patted his cheek, let her palm rest there, the gesture as light and teasing as Rayne's would have been.

Only Skylar wasn't Rayne, and the contact shot through Jonas like lightning through a stormy sky. Skylar felt it, too. Her breath caught, her pupils dilating as she let her hand drop away and stepped back.

"Remind me to give you the code tonight." His voice was gruff, his muscles tight as he grabbed juice from the fridge, poured her a glass. "Drink."

She eyed him over the rim as he phoned the security company, her gaze uneasy and unsure.

Funny. That was exactly how he felt

Or maybe it wasn't so funny.

He hung up, tried to focus his thoughts.

"I just spoke to Sheriff Smithson. His office is taking over the investigation from the Phoenix P.D. since you were abducted from their jurisdiction. He'd like to interview both of us. He also said he has some of your things. You're free to pick them up when you're ready."

"I'm ready." She set the empty glass in the sink, brushing past him as she walked out of the kitchen. Just a hint of contact, but Jonas felt it to his core.

He frowned, grabbing his keys and wallet, tossing a jacket

in Skylar's direction. She pulled it on, hurried to the door, as eager to escape, it seemed, as Jonas was.

By the time he'd locked the door, she was in the truck, her jean-clad legs and boot-encased feet disappearing as she shut the door.

"What did you think of the sheriff?" Skylar asked after Jonas had climbed into the truck and started the engine. Jonas met her eyes. Wished he hadn't. Everything she felt was written there. Trepidation. Confusion. Curiosity.

It was the curiosity that might get them both in deeper than either wanted to go. Especially since it was a trait he shared.

"Not much. He said he'd been keeping an eye on Redmond, but wouldn't answer when I asked who the guy's friends were. Where he hung out."

"Probably because he was tired of answering me when I asked."

"That's what he said."

"The thing is, I asked a dozen times in a dozen different ways, and all he'd say was that Redmond hung out at the diner where he worked, spent all his time with the people there. No specifics. No names."

"Maybe he's hiding something."

"Or he doesn't know and doesn't want to admit it. He's arrogant enough to think he knows everything about the people in Cave Creek. It might stick in his craw that he doesn't."

"It sounds like he didn't make much of an impression on you."

"Actually, he didn't. Not a good impression, and not a bad one, either. Which is unusual. When you're a cop, it helps to know the good guys from the bad ones. I've almost always been able to do it."

"*Almost* always?"

"There've been a few exceptions."

"Your partner?"

"Yes, though I did think something was up with him the last year we worked together. I thought maybe he was cheating on his wife. Turns out he was cheating on the department."

"Who else did you mistake for a good guy?" There it was. The curiosity. Pushing Jonas to find out more than he needed to.

"No one important."

"Which means he was."

"I never said it was a 'he.'"

"But it *was* a man, right?"

"If you can call the kind of guy Matthew was a *man,* then yeah." She crossed her arms over her chest, closed in and off in a way he'd never seen her before.

"You dated?"

"We were engaged."

"You didn't make it to the altar, so I guess you saw him for what he was."

"It's hard not to see something when it's right in front of your face."

"What happened?"

"How about we change the subject?"

"This one was just getting interesting."

"I can think of some that would interest me more."

"Like?"

"One of the nurses said you were a Shadow Wolf."

"And?"

"Were you?"

"I told you I was a border patrol agent."

"Why'd you give it up?"

"Guilt. My wife and son's murders were a paid hit, revenge against me for confiscating a few hundred thousand dollars' worth of cocaine and throwing half a dozen gang members in jail. My job cost my family their lives. It wasn't a good trade-off." Old news, but it still hurt to say it.

"So, they won."

"Who?"

"The gang."

"No. We closed them down. I made sure of that before I quit."

"Glad to hear it, but since they succeeded in getting a successful agent off the playing field, I'm not sure it was a total loss for them."

"If you're trying to make me feel better, it's not working." He bit the words out as he pulled up in front of the sheriff's department, yanked the keys from the ignition.

"Why would I do that? You suffered a great loss, Jonas. No doubt about that, but throwing away all the good you did, all the good you *could* do, I don't think that's the answer to your grief or your guilt," she shot back.

"You have no idea what you're talking about." The words were as icy as the cold fury that pulsed through him. He'd had a lot of people say a lot of things about the tragedy, but Skylar was the first to say that he'd let the gang win.

He didn't like it.

And right at that moment, he didn't much like *her.*

"Maybe not. But if I had a choice, I'd be back on the force, throwing the book at the drug dealing scum who hook people in, shoot them up with lies and poison and then steal everything they have. Unfortunately, the powers that be are worried that I'm a medical risk. They sat me at a desk job for three months after my recovery, and desk jobs just aren't my thing." Her smile was brittle, and Jonas's fury seeped out as quickly as it had come. She had her own pain, her own loss.

"Skylar—"

"What you do is a God-given gift, Jonas. But it's not my business if you waste it. I'm sorry I brought it up. Come on.

I need to get my things and focus on finding Redmond, so we can both get back to our lives." She got out of the truck and was halfway across the parking lot before Jonas opened his door.

A God-given gift.

They were the same words Rayne had used.

There'd been a time when Jonas had believed that. A time when he'd truly felt that his ability to track and his success on the field were God-given. Gabriella had believed the same, and her support had only added to the feeling. For the last few years, though, all Jonas had felt was his loss.

Skylar was right. Throwing everything away, changing careers, giving up what he loved hadn't healed his grief or assuaged his guilt.

All it had done was leave him empty.

He frowned, holding the door open as Skylar stepped into the building. She'd said she needed to get to work so they could get back to their lives, but he wasn't sure he wanted to go back to what he'd spent the past four years being. It was something to think about, anyway. Maybe even to pray about. It's what Gabriella would have wanted, and he let the thought warm him as he followed Skylar into the sheriff's department.

TEN

She should have kept her mouth shut.

Should have.

But she hadn't.

Apparently, she loved the sensation of opening it and inserting her foot.

And, apparently, she also loved seeing the fury in people's eyes when she stuck her nose into things that were absolutely none of her business.

She sighed, her heart thumping painfully as she approached the reception desk and greeted the deputy who sat there.

"I'm—"

"Skylar Grady. I'd recognize you from your photos even if we hadn't met before." He smiled, his deeply tanned face and short cropped hair vaguely familiar. She must have questioned him when she had arrived in town.

"I'm sorry. The past few days have been crazy. I guess I forgot that we'd met."

"I'm Deputy Marcus Williams. We spoke for about two minutes the day you arrived in Cave Creek, but I wasn't in uniform, so don't beat yourself up about it." He stood. "The sheriff was hoping you'd get here before his meeting. I'll take you back to his office."

"Thanks." She followed him through a door and into the corridor beyond, Jonas close on her heels. He hadn't said a word since they'd left the truck.

Not that she'd given him time.

She'd run like a coward, and she still wasn't ready to meet his eyes.

What had she been thinking?

They were strangers, and his life was his business.

But he hadn't felt like a stranger when he'd led her up the mesa or down into the desert. Hadn't felt like one when he'd prodded her to keep going through one of the longest nights of her life, or when he'd handed her clothes to borrow, or covered her with an afghan after she'd fallen asleep at Rayne's computer. He'd felt like someone who cared, and that made Skylar want to care, too.

And when she cared, she sometimes cared too much.

Which was another ailment that she couldn't seem to cure herself of.

Deputy Williams knocked on the sheriff's door, pushed it open and gestured for them to walk inside.

"Good to see you alive and kicking, Skylar." A tall broad-shouldered man greeted them as they stepped into the room. Silver-haired, with steel gray eyes, Sheriff Rodger Smithson looked ready for battle, his uniform spotless, his boots polished. And despite the cordiality of his greeting, his eyes blazing.

Obviously, he wasn't happy that she hadn't left town when he'd told her to. In his opinion, a week of questioning the locals with no results was plenty.

Skylar hadn't agreed.

Still didn't.

"It's good to *be* alive and kicking."

"I bet. Go ahead and take a seat. I have a dinner meeting

in twenty minutes, and I can't miss it. We need to cover a lot before then."

She perched on the edge of the chair, her leg so close to Jonas's they were almost touching. She tried to ignore him, as she reached for a folder the sheriff slid across the desk. "What's this?"

"All the evidence we've collected so far. It's not much, but it's a start."

She opened the folder, frowning at the two photos that lay on the top of the printed pages.

Three separate photos of three different scenes. Close-ups of bullets that lay spent on the ground. "Were these found in close proximity to one another?"

"Three of them were. The fourth was about a half mile away."

"It might not be related, then. I only remember three shots being fired."

"How about you, Jonas? Do you remember more than three shots being fired?

"No." He leaned in to look at the photos, his knee and arm pressing against Skylar's, his warmth seeping through the layers of jean and jacket. It was distracting—and it shouldn't have been. She spent a lot of time with men. Had plenty of guy friends from her days on the force that she still hung out with. She'd been hiking, climbing and camping with dozens of her buddies and she'd never been so aware, so completely and absolutely in tune with a man as she seemed to be with Jonas.

Every breath he took, she felt.

Every move, she noticed.

"One bullet is from my Glock. These other two look like they are from the pistol we took from one of the perps. Phoenix P.D. has it," Jonas offered, and Sheriff Smithson nodded.

"It was found in the location where you indicated a gun

had been fired. We're already doing ballistics testing on the gun. We'll let you know when we have the results. We've also traced its serial number to a hunting store outside of Phoenix. It was reported stolen a couple months ago. Could have been in anyone's hands."

"What about the fourth bullet?"

"Like I said, it was found a half mile away. We have trackers trying to follow a trail out there, but with all the rain we got last night, it's difficult."

"They found the bullets. They may find something else."

"Let's hope so. We need more if we're going to find out what's going on."

Skylar spread out the remainder of the file's contents. The sheriff was right. There wasn't much. A picture of her rental jeep. A copy of the missing person's report Kane had filed when she failed to check in with him. A photo of the hotel room she'd been staying in.

She lifted it, frowning as she studied the details. "When was this taken?"

"The day you were reported missing. Once we got notification that you'd missed a conference call with your employer, we sent someone to your hotel room. Took a few pictures just to be on the safe side, but didn't see anything that concerned us."

"Was the cleaning crew in before you got there?"

"That morning, but the crew said it looked just like you see it—clean."

"Then someone cleaned it before they got there. Three thugs broke into the room while I was sleeping, and I grabbed the lamp to protect myself. Slammed it into someone's head." She pointed to the porcelain lamp sitting untouched on a table beside the bed.

"Did it break?" Jonas asked, and she had no choice but to

meet his gaze, look into eyes that made her stomach flutter. She shoved the feeling down, forced herself not to look away.

"Yes. I tipped over the chair, too, trying to get out the door, but three against one weren't good odds, and I was shot full of dope before I could escape."

"Wish we'd have known all that six days ago. But the room was fine when the cleaning crew arrived. There were no reports of noise or a struggle." The sheriff frowned, jotting notes on a pad of paper.

"It's still possible a good forensic team could find something." Skylar had known plenty of cleaned crime scenes to yield evidence.

"We have a team there now. Problem is, cleaning services have been in and out of the room at least twice. We impounded your rental vehicle, and we'll check that, too. It hasn't been rented out again, so we have more hope of finding something there."

"How about Daniel Redmond? Have you located him?" Skylar asked, and the sheriff frowned.

"I have men searching his place. If Redmond left any clues as to his whereabouts, we'll find them."

"More than one person was gunning for Skylar. That being the case, it seems to me, your town has a bigger problem than a deadbeat dad who's gone missing. Who are Redmond's connections? What did he spend his time doing? You told me that you were keeping an eye on him. You must have noticed those things."

"Any information I have on that is part of the official investigation. For now all I can say is that we're checking into those things, and we're being thorough about it. The best thing either of you can do is go back to your lives, let us handle the investigation." The sheriff's face tightened, but other than that, he kept his irritation hidden.

"I can't do that, Sheriff," Skylar replied. "I came here

to track Redmond down. I'm not going to leave until I find him."

"I'm not surprised. Like I told your friend, you get hold of something, and you don't let it go. Keep this in mind, though." He leaned in, spearing her with steel gray eyes. "We've got our share of trouble in this area. Nice as it is, upscale as we keep it, we have drugs and illegal weapons and gangs and all manner of things that a person can fall into. Could be Redmond fell into that kind of trouble. If that's the case, it could be the people coming after you aren't the kind of people you want to be messin' with."

"I mess with all sorts of people, Sheriff. That's part of the job. So, I think I'll just stick around until Redmond shows up."

"I really don't recommend it. Just ask your friend if you don't believe that things can go real bad real fast. His wife got caught in the cross fire of a gang war."

"What happened to my wife has nothing to do with this case. There's no need to pull it out and wave it around as an example." Jonas leaned forward, his eyes blazing. Skylar put a hand on his shoulder, pressing him back before he could do what *she* wanted to and slam a fist into the sheriff's nose.

"I apologize. I didn't mean that to sound the way it did, and I didn't mean to cause you more pain than you've already suffered. What happened to your wife was a tragedy. I would just hate to see the same happen to Skylar. I guess my concern got the best of me." The sheriff smiled, but there was something hard in his gaze.

"Apology accepted but, just so you know, Skylar isn't the only one who plans to see this investigation through." Jonas stood. "I think we're about at the end of your twenty minutes."

"You're right. I do have to get going. I'll call you with updates, and you call me if you have any more trouble."

"I will. Thanks." Skylar stood, too, though she was reluctant to let things go so quickly. There was more she wanted to say. Plenty she wanted to ask. She'd worked as a police officer in New York, and she knew the way the system worked. Knew that the first forty-eight hours were the most important in any investigation.

No doubt Sheriff Smithson knew the same.

So, why wasn't he out in the desert spearheading the investigation?

Why didn't he have anything to share about Daniel Redmond?

Why was he sitting behind his desk allowing his men to work the case?

Why was going to a meeting more important than investigating an attempted murder?

She almost let the questions pop out, but Sheriff Smithson didn't seem like the kind of guy who'd appreciate being reminded of his priorities.

"All set?" Deputy Williams greeted them as they entered the reception area, a black suitcase sitting beside him. *Skylar's* black suitcase. She nearly cried with joy.

Clean clothes that fit. Shoes that didn't pinch blistered feet. And if they'd gotten her things from the Jeep, that meant she'd also have her wallet. Her laptop and cell phone. After nearly a week of being cut off from everyone and everything, she was finally getting her life back.

"Looks like you have my stuff."

"It's already too contaminated to yield any usable evidence, so you're welcome to take it. I put your purse and cell phone inside the suitcase. They were found in the jeep."

"Thanks."

"No problem. I'll take it out to your car for you."

"I'll get it." Jonas grabbed the case before the deputy could, his movements tight and short.

Still upset.

With the sheriff.

Maybe with Skylar.

She couldn't say she blamed him. He'd gone out of his way to help a friend, and he'd gotten nothing more than trouble for his efforts.

She followed him to the door, walking through as Deputy Williams held it open.

To her surprise, the deputy stepped outside, following them to Jonas's truck.

"Listen, the sheriff will have my head if he knows I let this leak, but there's something going on at Redmond's place, and I think you should know about it." Williams's quiet words made Skylar's heart leap, and she glanced around, made sure they were alone in the parking lot.

"What?"

"The evidence team found blood splatter on the bedroom wall. Wasn't visible to the naked eye. There's blood smeared on the wood floor, too. A trail of it leading to the backyard and a brand new cement slab."

"Are they pulling it up?" Jonas asked, his body seeming to hum with energy. The thrill of the chase, the exhilaration of gathering the clues and finding the answers, it didn't go away. Not when it was what a person was meant to do.

And Jonas was.

The fact that she shouldn't have said it, didn't make it untrue. He had a gift for tracking people, and she hated to see him wasting it.

"We started doing that an hour ago. The sheriff likes to keep things close to the cuff until he has all the facts. Otherwise, he wouldn't have hesitated to mention it."

"He keeps it close to the cuff, and you let the world know?" Jonas asked before Skylar could.

"You're both former law-enforcement agents. Both of you

have backgrounds in investigation. I don't see any reason to keep it from you. The fact is, Rodger and I are friends. We have cookouts together, golf together, hunt together. We get along just fine, but it's an election year, and I think that's influencing the way he's conducting this investigation."

"What do you mean?" Curious, Skylar studied the deputy. He seemed sincere, concerned, maybe even a little uncomfortable.

"Between what happened to you and what's been found at Redmond's place, it's obvious something big is going on. In light of that, Rodger should be hip deep in the investigation, not hanging out with his campaign manager. It's going to bite him in the butt if he's not careful. If you two start talking down about him, complaining that he's withholding information, that'll be another nail in the coffin. I don't want to see that happen." He frowned, obviously troubled by the thought.

"I appreciate the information, Deputy, but I don't make a habit of talking anyone down," Skylar reassured him, but his comments had made her even more curious about the sheriff and his priorities.

"Good to know. Keep your nose clean and watch your back. If you're murdered in Cave Creek after you made it through six days alone in the desert—"

"The sheriff will have a really bad election year?" she offered, and he smiled. Shook his head.

"That, too, but I'm more concerned about you. You've come too far and fought too hard to die on the street of our little town. So, be careful." He offered a quick wave and walked away.

"Do you think he's on the up and up?" Jonas asked, his gaze following the deputy's retreat.

"Why would he lie?"

"Why would anyone?" He lifted the suitcase into the truck bed.

"I don't know, but whatever his motivation, he's given us some interesting information, and I think we should move on it."

"I suppose you want to head over to Redmond's."

"I think we should."

We?

She didn't do *we*. Hadn't done *we* since her days working as a police officer and the betrayal that had nearly taken her life. Matthew's actions had only cemented her certainty that she was better off on her own. She'd made that clear to Kane when she'd accepted the job he'd offered.

Yet there she was, getting ready to check out a potential crime scene with Jonas.

She frowned, wishing she'd grabbed her cell phone from the suitcase. She could have charged the phone, made a call to Kane and let him know just how unhappy she was to have Jonas around.

Only she wasn't unhappy.

That was the truth, and she always tried to tell it. Even to herself.

Having Jonas around was…comforting.

Or maybe not.

Comforting was a warm fire on a cold day, a faithful old dog pattering through the house at night, the first rays of sun after a storm.

Jonas wasn't comforting.

He was excitement and anticipation and safety all rolled into one.

And that terrified her.

Everyone she'd ever loved had betrayed her in one way or another. Everyone she should have been able to count on had failed her. She didn't want to be disappointed or betrayed again. Not by anyone, but especially not by Jonas.

And that, she decided, was the most terrifying truth of all.

ELEVEN

Jonas pulled out of the parking lot, his body humming with anticipation. When he'd worked border patrol, the thrill of the hunt had driven him. The quick burst of adrenaline, the buzz of energy, he'd loved both, and he'd lived for them as much as he'd lived for almost anything. Looking back, he could see that that hadn't been healthy. If he ever went back to it, he'd do things differently. Keep balanced. Find thrills in everyday life as much as he'd found them in his job. Appreciate the quiet times as much as he did the action.

If he went back?

That he was actually considering it surprised him. Three years ago, he wouldn't have. One year ago, he wouldn't have.

Now?

He wasn't sure, but he was going to go with his instincts, follow them where they led. Instincts and God. Skylar had used those words to describe how she'd survived her partner's betrayal, and Jonas didn't doubt the truth of them. God existed. He had power to create and to save.

Could Jonas accept that God's ability to save didn't always mean that He would? Could he leave the fate of his loved ones to God's will, trusting in God's love even when His plan wasn't clear?

Jonas had learned faith from his grandfather, but the

truths Pops had tried to impart had poured off him like water on an oil slick. A fatherless kid with a mother who'd barely cared didn't spend much time thinking about eternity. At least, Jonas hadn't. Even after Pops had died and Jonas had moved in with his father and Debby, gone to church with them every time the doors were open, Jonas hadn't absorbed what he was being soaked in. Until he'd met Gabriella and watched the way she'd lived her convictions, he hadn't understood what true faith meant or strived to achieve it. Once she was gone, he hadn't cared enough to keep striving.

But maybe God hadn't stopped striving for him.

"Turn left here." Skylar broke into his thoughts, and he turned onto the street, parked a few houses away from Redmond's place. No question about which one it was. Police cars filled the driveway and lined the curb in front of it, and two officers stood at the front door.

"Think they'll be happy to see us?" she asked, as she got out of the truck.

"Not as happy as the sheriff was to see us go."

"He did seem anxious to get rid of us. Of course, that might have been because you looked like you were about to put your fist through his face."

"I thought about it."

"So did I. Listen." She grabbed his arm, soft curls tumbling past her collarbone, the neckline of her sweater revealing half an inch of purple scar. "I want to apologize again for what I said earlier. I should have kept my mouth shut."

"Is that something you do often?"

"Keep my mouth shut? I'm afraid not."

"Don't start doing it on my account, then."

"I really do regret hurting you. You know that, right?"

"You didn't hurt me."

"Don't lie to make me feel better." She touched his shoulder, warmth seeping through his jacket, heating his skin and speeding his pulse. He'd be carried away by his feelings if he wasn't careful. Start thinking about things that couldn't be, or shouldn't. Like risking it all again, like letting himself believe he could build something different than what he'd had with Gabriella, but something just as strong and wonderful.

"I'm not in the habit of lying to make anyone feel better. Come on. Let's see if those officers will tell us what's been found." He walked to the house, catching his breath, refocusing his thoughts.

One of the officers stepped forward. "Sorry, folks, you're going to have to leave."

"I'm Skylar Grady. I'm a private investigator from New York, in town looking for Daniel Redmond."

"I recognize you. Your face has been plastered on the front page of the local newspaper for almost a week. You're also the reason we've spent half the day searching this property."

"Then you understand why I'm interested in knowing what you've found."

"I understand it, but it's not my place to give out any information." The deputy shoved up sunglasses onto her head, a frown line between her brows.

"But a male body *was* found, right?" Jonas took a stab in the dark, and the deputy cocked her head, studied him for a moment.

"I guess it can't hurt to say. The news hounds have been sniffing around all morning, so I'm sure everyone in town will know by this afternoon. Someone *is* dead. We haven't identified who, yet."

"There's no doubt the victim was a man?"

"None. No doubt about how he died, either. Guy was shot execution style. Arms tied behind his back, bullet to the back of the head. Slashed throat. Not pretty, even after the body's been buried for weeks."

"How many?"

"Weeks? That's for the medical examiner to say, but I'd guess three or four based on the condition of the body." The deputy tapped her fingers against her thigh, scanning the yard.

"That coincides with the time frame of Redmond's disappearance," Jonas said, wishing he had the right to cross the yard, look down into the open grave. See the victim for himself.

"That's another thing that will have to be decided by the medical examiner. If it is Redmond, he was involved with some bad stuff. These kinds of crimes are usually gang related."

"It's not very common for a gang member to bury a victim. The goal of the killing is usually to advertise power and bravado. Even a revenge killing is meant to show that. Why hide it?" Skylar asked, her gaze jumping to Jonas.

"Good questions, but I'm afraid I can't answer them. I've only been with the Cave Creek Sheriff's department for a few months, so I'm serving as guard rather than investigator today," the deputy responded.

"Who's in charge of the investigation?"

"Should be the sheriff, but he hasn't shown up yet. Samuel Mitchell is taking the lead until he arrives."

"May we speak with him?"

"It's no skin off my back if you do, but I'm not sure he'll agree to it." She opened the front door, called inside. "Hey, Sam! There are some people here who'd like to speak with you."

"If they're reporters, I don't have time." The sharp response came moments before a man stepped into view. Midthirties. A little under six feet. Looked like he'd recently come out of the military.

"What's up?"

"Chief Deputy Samuel Mitchell, this is Skylar Grady and…" She paused, apparently realizing Jonas had never offered his name.

"Jonas Sampson." He extended a hand, and Mitchell shook it, studying Jonas's face as if he was sure they'd met before. It wasn't an uncommon reaction. Losing his wife and unborn son in such a tragic way had made Jonas headline news for a few days. Many people remembered his face, though they couldn't place where they'd seen it.

"Sounds familiar."

"I've restored a dozen homes in Cave Creek." It was as likely an explanation as any, and the chief deputy seemed satisfied with.

"That could be it. What can I do for you folks?"

"I'm trying to close a case that I've been working on for the past month. Daniel Redmond is wanted for back child support, and his wife hired the PI service I work for to find him. We're wondering if he might be the man you found here."

"This isn't information I want released to the press, but maybe it will help you close your case a little more quickly. One of our men is confident that the deceased is Daniel Redmond."

"Any reason for that?" Jonas asked.

"He pulled Redmond over for speeding once, said the guy was wearing a watch like the one the deceased has on."

"Lots of people wear watches."

"This is an expensive one. Some fancy Italian maker."

"So, it's very possible Daniel Redmond is dead." Skylar seemed to be speaking more to herself than anyone else, and Jonas could almost see her mind working.

Who had murdered Daniel?

What did his murder have to do with the attempt on Skylar's life?

"We'll check dental records to confirm it. We're also going to have the medical examiner get fingerprints if possible. If Redmond has a record—"

"He does. His wife reported him for abuse, and he was booked in New York three years ago," Skylar broke in, but she sounded distracted, her skin pale beneath the sunburn.

"Then we shouldn't have any trouble confirming his identity."

"I've seen several photos of Redmond. I'd be happy to take a look at the victim. See if I can identify him."

"He's pretty beat up. The bullet went in through the back of the head and exploded on its way out the other side. Destroyed a good portion of his face. A visual identification isn't going to do it."

"The sheriff has my contact information. Can you give me a call when you know for sure?" Skylar persisted, and the deputy nodded.

"No problem. Now if you'll excuse me, I have to get back to work." He hurried away, and Skylar scowled.

"Well, that told us just about nothing."

"It told us that Redmond is probably dead."

"Which means he wasn't out in the desert last night, he didn't hire a posse to kill me. If he didn't, who did?"

"The person who killed him?"

"It makes sense, but until we know what kind of trouble Redmond was involved in, there's no way of knowing who that person might be." She sighed, shoved a bundle of curls back behind her ear. "It's times like this when I really wish I had my badge back."

"You think they'd let you view the burial site if you did?"

"If I were investigating a criminal case against Redmond, they would. Of course, I doubt being back there would do me any good. Seeing him dead won't tell me who murdered him, but having my badge would force Smithson to share what he knows."

"Maybe we can get the information another way. You've spoken with Redmond's coworkers, right?"

"Until we were all just about sick of it. No one knew anything of importance."

"News about the body is going to spread fast. Whether the remains belong to Redmond or not, people are going to assume he's the one buried behind his house. Friends and coworkers might view the past differently in light of what they know about the present, and they might be willing to share their new insight."

"You have a point. Let's head over to the diner. See if we can—"

"Sorry to ruin your plans, Grady, but we're not going anywhere but home." He motioned for her to climb into the truck, rounded the vehicle and started the engine.

"Since when do you get the deciding vote on our plans?" she asked as he pulled away from the crime scene.

"Since I saw how pale you were."

"I'm fine."

"It's getting dark, and we're both running on empty. We need to get a few hours of sleep and come at the investigation fresh once we're thinking more clearly."

"Maybe you're right."

"It's been known to happen."

She smiled, the expression sweet and sad all at the same time.

"What's wrong?"

"You. You're not like the other guys I know, and I'm finding it difficult to pretend you are."

"Who says you have to?"

"What if I don't? What then?"

"Then, we go with it, and we see where it takes us." His

response came easily, quickly, and he knew it was right. Knew it was what Gabriella would want for him. Knew it was what he'd want for her if their situations were reversed. He couldn't commit to a relationship—wasn't sure if he could handle it, if he was prepared for the risks. But ignoring the connection both of them were feeling wasn't doing any good. For now he wanted to see where it led them. Go with it and let himself feel, just a little, again.

"Now *you're* upset." Skylar's fingers brushed his biceps, her touch light and tentative.

"No. I'm just thinking that I understand your fear. I know what it's like to love and lose and even to be betrayed. I never want to hurt again like I hurt after my wife and son were murdered, but I wouldn't give up the years I had with Gabriella to save myself the pain. Sometimes we have to be willing to risk everything to have something wonderful."

"And sometimes we risk everything to have something we think is wonderful and realize it's only a poor reflection of our dreams, a vague likeness of everything we hoped for. Not something we can touch or feel or hold on to. Then, we've risked it all for nothing." She turned away, and he knew he should let it be. Let her be.

"The guy who hurt you? He was a fool, Skylar. You know that, don't you?"

"Yes, but I was the bigger fool. I don't want to be that again."

"Sky—"

"Look, I'm so tired the world is spinning, and if I'm not careful, I'll spin away with it. How about we finish this conversation another time?" She closed her eyes, and this time, he let silence fill the car.

There was nothing more he could say. After all, Skylar wasn't the only one who was afraid to risk her heart. As much as she intrigued him, as much as he wanted to know more about her, he couldn't shake the fear that was just beneath the surface when he was with her.

What if he *did* risk it all?

And what if he lost it all again?

What if he failed the same way he'd failed before?

What then?

Would he look back and know that it had all been worth the pain? Or would he live the rest of his life regretting what he had lost?

He didn't know, but he half believed he was ready to find out.

For now the investigation had to take priority.

Everything else would follow.

If he could keep Skylar alive. Keep himself alive.

A tall order when a posse of men was hunting them.

A posse that meant business.

At least one man was already dead.

He and Skylar needed to find out why. It was the key to discovering everything else. With that in mind, Jonas pulled out his phone and dialed Kane's number.

TWELVE

"Grady?" The masculine voice drifted into Skylar's dreams. She wanted to ignore it. Would have if the speaker hadn't touched her shoulder, shaken her gently.

Once.

Twice.

The third time was too jarring to ignore, and she opened one eye, shot Jonas a look she hoped would send him running. "Go away."

"Is that any way to talk to the guy who spent three days combing the desert, searching for you?"

"It is when he just woke me from a sound sleep. I don't like people who wake me up."

"You'd like me less if I left you sleeping in the car while Kane and I discussed the best way to get you out of danger." He said, dangling a cell phone in front of her face, then pulling it back when she reached for it.

"She's awake, Kane. I'm going to get her into the apartment before I put her on the phone. No sense tempting fate by sitting out in the car." He grabbed her suitcase, tucked the phone into his pocket.

"I can walk and talk at the same time, you know," Skylar grumbled as she tumbled out of the truck, barely managing to keep from falling.

"You've yet to prove it." He laughed, wrapping an arm around her waist, hurrying her into the apartment and turning off the alarm.

"Okay. We're safe and sound. Now hand me that phone. I've been waiting for a week to give Kane a piece of my mind. That's a whole lot of pent-up angst." She snatched the phone from his hand, pressed it to her ear. "You said this was going to be an easy assignment."

"I should have known it wouldn't be, since you agreed to take it." Kane's gruff response made her smile, and she settled onto the couch, tucked her knees up close to her chest and rested her head on them.

"Thanks for sending the cavalry."

"Are you still giving him trouble?"

"Actually, he's still giving me trouble." She shot Jonas a look, lost her train of thought as he moved across the room, all lean, hard muscle and grace.

"Not a surprise. You're two of the most stubborn people I've ever met. I'm shocked you haven't killed each other yet."

"I've been tempted, but I don't want to waste the energy. There are more important things I need to expend it on."

"So I hear. Looks like Redmond is dead."

"Looks like it."

"Which means your investigation is over."

"Not until I find out who killed him, and who is trying to kill me."

"That's the job of the police, Skylar. Leave it to them."

"You know I'm not going to do that, right?"

"Then investigate from New York. I already paid for a ticket. The flight is leaving in three hours. Jonas has agreed to drive you to the airport and wait with you until your plane takes off."

"Traitor." She mouthed the words and Jonas shrugged, pulling a soda from the fridge and popping the lid.

"You still there, Skylar?"

"Yes and I plan to be here three hours from now, too."

"You're getting on the plane. That's an order."

"One I'm not going to follow, boss."

"You know I hate when you call me that."

"Which is exactly why I do it."

"Stop trying to change the subject."

"I don't see any need to continue it."

"I may not like you calling me boss, but it's what I am. I need you back in New York. There are cases piling up, and you're the one I want to handle them."

"I haven't taken a vacation in two years. Consider this mine."

"If I weren't so relieved you were alive, I'd fire you for being insubordinate."

"And if I didn't know you had a dozen investigators who could take those cases, I would get on a plane and handle things for you."

"A dozen investigators, but none of them are as good as you." All the amused irritation in his voice was gone, and she could imagine him pacing his office, worry etching lines on his face. She'd met Kane the day his son had disappeared, had been the first officer to respond to the nanny's frantic 9-1-1 call. A rookie cop, she'd been the one to reassure Kane, the one who'd told him how few children were abducted by strangers. They'd searched the neighborhood park together, and she'd seen his worry grow to panic as dusk settled over the city and his son was still not home. They'd formed a bond that day, one that had carried them through Kane's years of anguished searching, through Skylar's painful recovery, her breakup and, finally, into Kane's new beginning. She loved him like a brother, and as much as she enjoyed sparring with him, she hated to see him worried.

"If you're complimenting me, you must really be worried. You shouldn't be. I have everything under control."

"I have plenty to worry about. Jonas said there were at least ten men hunting you last night. Ten against one doesn't seem fair. As a matter of fact, it seems like overkill."

"I guess they wanted to make sure they got the job done."

"Not they. Whoever is in charge. The same person who put the hit on Redmond. I've done a little research on the guy. He's been in some trouble before. Got kicked out of his teaching position at the university for passing off a student's research as his own."

"He was accused of the same at another university, but they couldn't prove it, and he walked." She'd gotten the information from Redmond's ex but hadn't looked any further into the incident. There'd been no need before.

Now she was going to dig up every aspect of the man's life. With Kane and the rest of the Information Unlimited team, it wouldn't be difficult.

"He taught archeology, right?" Kane asked.

"That and ancient studies. His ex-wife said he had doctorates in both."

"Smart guy."

"Not smart enough to stay out of trouble."

"Or to stay alive. Does anyone in Cave Creek know who would want him dead?"

"Not anyone who is willing to admit it. Yet. Tomorrow, Jonas and I are going to question his coworkers. The way I figure it, someone somewhere knows something. It's just a matter of finding out who."

"Just be sure you don't make more enemies in the process."

"That would be hard to do, seeing as how I'm sweet as sugar and twice as nice."

"Right." Kane snorted, and the soft sound of a baby's cry

drifted into Skylar's ear. "Now you've done it, Skylar. You've made me wake up the kid."

"Don't blame me. You're the one who snorted loud enough to scare her out of a sound sleep."

"Hold on." He murmured something Skylar couldn't hear, and she could imagine him looking down at his baby girl. Imagine the son he'd thought he'd lost standing beside them. His wife hovering in the background, waiting for him to get off the phone.

Kane had changed in the years since he'd been reunited with his little boy. He'd married, had another child, softened in an indefinable way. It was the stuff dreams were made of, and Skylar didn't want to take away from his contentment, didn't want to add worry to his life.

"Sorry about that."

"No problem. Why don't I let you go back to your family and—"

"Not so fast, Skylar. Like I was saying, I have plenty to worry about. You've stepped into something messy, and until we know what it is, we've got no way of cleaning it up. I don't want you taking needless chances. I don't want you hurt."

"I've been hurt before and lived to tell the tale, Kane. You know that."

"I also know you're not a cat. You don't have nine lives, and that second chance you got last time? It might have been your last."

"You worry too much."

"Only because I'm good at it. And now I do have to go. Be careful and check in with me when you have new information."

"I will."

"And don't kill Jonas. I'm trying to talk him into joining the team."

"Yeah?"

"He'd be good at it."

"He'd be better at his old job."

"If you two are planning to talk about me, I'll take the phone and help you finish the conversation," Jonas spoke up, his head bent over a chopping board as he sliced onions and green peppers.

"No need. We're done." Skylar said goodbye to Kane and handed the phone to Jonas, her stomach growling as she caught a whiff of onion. "Thanks."

"For lending you the phone?"

"For cooking. Assuming you're planning to share whatever you make."

"I'm starving, so I'd like to refuse and keep it all for myself, but my grandfather raised me right."

"Your grandfather, not your father and Debby?"

"I moved in with them when I was fifteen. I didn't even know my father existed until then. Pops died. My mother was arrested for drunk and disorderly, and the next thing I knew, I had a father, a stepmother and a baby sister."

"Must have been shocking."

"You could say that." He cracked eggs into a bowl, scrambled them. "You want to toss some bread into the toaster? I'm making omelets."

"It seems like things worked out pretty well for all of you." She grabbed a loaf of bread and a stick of butter, sidling past Jonas as she headed for the toaster, realizing too late just how close that brought them. Hip to hip. Shoulder to shoulder. Arm to arm.

"They did. Thanks to Debby. She's one of the most understanding people I've ever met, and she was eager to make us into a family. She was more a mother to me than mine was before she died." He poured the eggs into a hot pan, leaning close as he grabbed a spatula from the drawer in front of Skylar.

Galley kitchens weren't made for two.

The longer she stood next to Jonas, the more sure of it Skylar was.

One person alone. Fine.

Two people together.

Not good.

She abandoned the toast, ready to escape to the living room, but Jonas blocked her path. "No need to run away, Skylar. I'm not going to bite."

"It's not biting I'm worried about," she muttered, grabbing hot toast and buttering it.

"Then what are you worried about?"

"You. Me. Standing in a kitchen that is only big enough for one."

"It feels plenty big enough to me." He slid an oversize omelet onto a plate, cut it in half. "But then, I'm not all that concerned about how close we're standing."

"I'm not, either." Not much anyway. "I just don't think this is a good idea." She dropped slices of toast on plates, shoved them toward Jonas.

"What?"

"Us cooking together. Being domestic. It feels too…"

"Intimate?"

"Something like that."

"Maybe you're just thinking about things wrong." He slid half the omelet onto each plate.

"Jonas—"

"Look, I'm not going to claim that I know where this is going, but I'm not going to deny that there's something between us, either."

"There's no—" She stopped short of denying it. Stopped short of looking him in the eye and lying.

To protect herself.

Her heart.

"Thanks." He patted her hand, lifted one of the plates.

"For what?"

"Not denying it, because ignoring it won't make it go away any more than acknowledging it will make it more than what it is. Maybe neither of us is ready for anything serious, but maybe we are. How will we know if we don't take the chance and see where this is going to lead?

"This—" Skylar lifted her plate, smiled past the sudden lump in her throat "—is going to lead to a full stomach."

"Do you always joke when you're afraid?" He didn't move aside when she tried to leave the kitchen. Just stood where he was, blocking her path, demanding that she face the same truth he had.

"I'm not afraid." This time, she did lie. He knew it. She knew it. She dropped her plate onto the counter, frustrated with herself, with him, with all the things that she shouldn't be feeling. "Okay. I am. Very afraid. I don't want to pull out all those old dreams, dust them off, start to believe in them again and then have them crushed."

"How do you know they will be?" He placed his plate next to hers, the food forgotten and going cold.

"Every dream I've ever had has been. Why would this time be any different?"

"Because this time, it's you and me and those dreams, and maybe we can make them come true." He cupped her face in his hands, leaned down so that their breath mingled, their gazes locked. She couldn't look away, couldn't move away.

Didn't even want to.

It felt so right standing there with him.

So good.

She could almost believe that things *would* be different with Jonas.

Almost.

Someone moved. Skylar. Jonas. She didn't know which. Didn't care. Their lips met, his hands drifting to the back of her head, sliding through her hair. She wound her arms around his waist, let herself be lost in the moment, because this was Jonas, and as much as Skylar didn't want to be hurt, she wanted to know *this*. How it felt to be in his arms, to touch silky hair, to feel the cold empty place in her heart fill until there was no room left for doubt, or worry, or nerves.

"I better go." He stepped back, his eyes blazing, and Skylar nodded. Didn't try to stop him as he opened the apartment door.

"I'm setting the alarm. If you need to leave, the code is 0-3-3-1, but call me before you go out. I don't want you wandering around outside without protection. My number is on the phone's contact list."

"You didn't eat your omelet." She picked up a plate, held it out.

Didn't eat your omelet?

It was only one of the lamest things she'd ever said.

He'd kissed her.

Or she'd kissed him.

Or, maybe, they'd kissed each other.

And now he was leaving, because what was between them was more than either of them had expected.

That being the case, Skylar figured the occasion deserved a lot more than mindless chatter about an omelet.

"I'll make another one at home." He didn't take the plate, and she knew what he was thinking.

One touch, one brush of hand against hand, and they'd be back in each other's arms, rushing headlong into something neither of them was quite ready for.

"Okay. Have a good night."

Lame.

Lame, lame, lame, lame.

Lame!

She could almost hear Tessa's chiding laughter, imagined her older sister rolling her eyes at Skylar's attempt at easy conversation.

Jonas stepped outside and closed the door, left her standing with the plate held out to an empty room.

She set it on the counter, disgusted to see that her hands were shaking.

Shaking!

Because of a kiss.

She needed to pull herself together.

Sure, Jonas had saved her life. Sure, he was one of the most compelling men she'd ever met. Maybe *the* most compelling man she'd ever met. That didn't mean she should lose her mind over him.

Too late. I already have.

The thought whispered through her head, and she tamped it down, grabbing one of the plates and diving into the omelet. She'd eat, sleep. When she woke up, she'd have a clearer perspective, a little more control.

She hoped.

Because the cold empty place in her heart, the one that had grown larger with every betrayal, emptier with every broken promise, it *was* filling. With a man who was larger than life and too good to be true, and all the things she knew made for a bad ending. Because larger than life usually meant small inside, and anything that seemed too good to be true, probably was.

Besides, she'd never come out on top in matters of the heart.

But maybe this time she would.

Because she'd grown up a lot in the past two years since she'd broken up with Matthew. She'd learned a lot. And maybe she was ready to try it all again. Reaching for the dream, striving for the happily-ever-after.

Maybe.

But she was too tired to know, too worn out to make any decision, and Jonas's kiss was still on her lips, warm and gentle and undemanding, all the things a kiss had never, ever been before.

She sighed, unzipping her suitcase and pulling out her cell phone. She plugged it into the charger, then spent a few minutes going through her notes on the case. Her mind refused to focus, though, and she grabbed her Bible, hoping to lose herself in scripture.

Hoping, but unsuccessful.

Her vision blurred, and she gave up, placing the Bible back in her suitcase and dropping onto the bed. She closed her eyes, thanking God for seeing her through another day, praying for guidance and protection, praying that she'd understand His will. Praying until her thoughts spun away, the silent words spinning with them as she tumbled into sleep.

Jonas stared out the living-room window, the soft tick of the grandfather clock he'd made for Gabriella the year they were married a rhythmic backdrop to his thoughts.

Three in the morning, and he was awake.

No light.

No television.

Nothing to distract him.

For once, that was the way he wanted it.

Kissing Skylar wasn't something he'd planned, but it had happened, and it had shaken him.

Deeply.

The heat, the passion, the connection he'd felt had been as unexpected as her response, her easy sinking into the embrace. He'd wanted more of her, more of that moment, more of what was building between them. Wanted it enough to know that he had to step away, give them both some space and some time to think.

And he *had* been thinking.

About the past.

About the future.

About possibilities that he couldn't have entertained a year ago.

He walked to the fireplace mantel, lifted a framed photo, stared down into Gabriella's face. "I know what you'd say, Gabby. You'd say, 'Be happy, Jonas. Live your life with joy. Don't hold my memory so close to your heart that you can't let anything else inside.'"

He could almost hear her voice, could almost feel her standing beside him, smell her flowery perfume. She had loved without reserve. Always. And she would want him to do the same.

Always.

He sighed, set the photograph back in its place.

Four years, and he still loved Gabriella, still mourned her and Simon, but maybe there was room for other things.

Contentment.

Peace.

Love.

Maybe there was room for other people.

Room for Skylar.

Maybe.

Probably.

Acknowledging that hurt, but not as much as ignoring it would.

He couldn't ignore the truth. No matter how difficult it was to swallow. He turned away from the photo, dropped onto the sofa, bowed his head and prayed as he hadn't done in years. For wisdom, for peace, for courage as he walked into whatever future God had planned for him.

THIRTEEN

Skylar's phone rang at four a.m., the sound seeping into her nightmares, pulling her from restless sleep. She jumped from the bed, nearly slamming into the wall as she raced into the living room and pulled her cell from the charger.

"Hello?" Still half-asleep, she shouted into the phone, wincing at the raw, rough sound of her voice echoing through the silent apartment.

"Skylar? It's Samuel Mitchell. Sorry for calling you so early."

"It's okay. What's up?"

"We've been able to match dental records and finger-prints, and we've confirmed our murder victim's identity. It's Daniel Redmond."

"That doesn't surprise me." She turned on a light, started the coffeemaker. She needed caffeine and she needed it fast, because Samuel Mitchell's early morning call wasn't making sense. They'd all assumed the identity of the victim. It wouldn't have hurt for him to wait a few more hours to give her the news.

"That's not why I'm calling, though."

Okay. So, there *was* more.

Good, because, she'd been sleeping in a comfortable bed

for the first time in weeks, and being pulled out of it hadn't made her happy.

"What is?" She fished an antibiotic tablet from the bottle the nurse had given her, popped it in her mouth, her hands shaky with the remnants of sleep and the fever she could still feel coursing through her.

"The tracking team discovered a body late last night. About six miles from the mesa and the bullet the team found yesterday."

Another body?

Suddenly, her thoughts were clear, all the sleepiness gone, the shakes dissipated as adrenaline started to flow. "Who is it?"

"An older guy. Five-eight, maybe a hundred and twenty pounds. Gray hair pulled into a braid. Hasn't been dead for more than thirty hours."

"Could be the elements got the best of him."

"The bullet in the back of his head and the slit in his throat say different."

"Same as Redmond?"

"Exactly. Sampson mentioned an older guy during his interview with Phoenix P.D., said the guy took a shot at you."

"That's right."

"Did you get a look at him?"

"Yes. From your description, I'd say it's the same guy. Wiry, older and the size fits. Do you have an identity on the victim?"

"Fortunately, yes. He's a career criminal named Josiah Stanley. Small-time thug. Liked to cash bad checks and shoplift. Got caught with marijuana a few times. Nothing big enough to get him put away for much time, but enough that we know his face and his name."

"So, he moved up on the crime ladder, messed with the big dogs and got himself killed?"

"Looks that way, but circumstantial evidence is only that. It's possible his death isn't connected to what happened to you."

"Not very."

"True, but we want proof positive if we can get it. That'll assure us that, once we find him, the person responsible will pay for all of his crimes."

"You want me to try to identify the body? That'll link everything for sure." Though she wasn't sure she could do it. She'd seen the guy in the dark and in a panic. Not good circumstances for taking in details.

"That won't be necessary, but we would like you and Sampson to look at some mug shots. If you can pick the deceased out of the lineup, that'll link things. We're also pulling prints, seeing if we can match his to ones found on the gun you carried out of the desert."

"I'm sure you'll find more of mine and Jonas's than anyone's. We weren't exactly worrying about contaminating evidence."

"We matched the ones belonging to both of you, and we have two others that we're running through the system."

"When do you want us to come to the station?"

"Whenever you're ready. We've already pulled the mug shots."

"You'll be there for a while?"

"A couple more hours."

"Then, I guess there's no time like the present."

"See you soon." He hung up, and Skylar grabbed clean clothes, took a quick shower and braided her hair, stared at the phone as she sipped a cup of coffee.

Call him.

She knew she had to, but if she let herself she could still feel the warmth of Jonas's lips, feel her senses tumbling into that place where nothing mattered. Where fear didn't exist and hurt couldn't intrude.

Where dreams might really come true.

A dangerous place to be, but there were bigger dangers she needed to be worried about, real fears that needed to concern her.

She grabbed the phone, found his number and dialed. Let it ring until voice mail picked up, and she left a message.

Was he still asleep?

If so, he'd earned the right, but Skylar's sleepiness had fled, caffeine and adrenaline making her restless for action.

She paced to the window, the minutes ticking by as she stared out into the dark morning. A shadow moved, easing around the side of Jonas's house, merging into the night. Gone as quickly as it was there.

Skylar's heart jumped, her pulse pounding in her ears as she watched, waited.

There! At the edge of Jonas's porch. Movement she might have missed if she weren't looking for it. Furtive. Slow. Disappearing around the corner of the house.

She grabbed the phone, called Jonas again. No answer. He slept while danger stalked, and Skylar wasn't going to wait around for it to reach him. She dialed the police, asking for backup as she grabbed a knife from the kitchen drawer, turned off the alarm and the lights. Quick, decisive, the way she'd been when she was on the force and every second counted, because every second *did* count.

Out the door, keeping low, sticking to shadows as she rounded the side of the house, the knife clutched in her hand. She wanted her gun, wished she'd carried it with her from New York. Too much trouble for an easy case, and she'd left it behind.

Hopefully, she'd live to regret her mistake.

No sirens, yet, and Skylar eased toward the back of the

house, listening, watching. Nothing. No movement. No sound. Just her quiet breaths, her crunching footsteps, her pounding heart.

Had she imagined the shadow? Imagined the movement?

She had a split second of doubt, and then he was on her, a shadow swooping in from nowhere, grabbing her wrist before she could move. The knife falling from numb fingers, as she was whipped around, pressed into the side of the house.

"Are you nuts?" Jonas hissed, his hand pressed to her mouth so that she couldn't respond, the faint sound of sirens ringing through the darkness.

Soft footfalls sounded near the back of the house, gravel crunching, someone running. Toward them? Away from them?

"Get down and stay down."

She barely had time to register the words before she was on the ground, lying in a winter dry flower bed as Jonas moved toward the back of the house. Lying in the dirt while he saved the day, and she didn't even know how she'd gotten there.

She reached for the knife and followed, trying to move as silently as Jonas. Failing miserably.

An engine roared to life, the sound shattering the stillness, lights flashing from a point beyond Jonas's driveway as a car sped away.

The *enemy* sped away.

Skylar sprinted to the road, nearly barreling into Jonas as she reached it.

He turned, grabbing her arm as she stopped short.

"I told you to stay down!" he growled over the sound of the approaching sirens.

"And you thought I would listen?"

"I thought you'd use some commonsense and stay in the

apartment instead of throwing yourself into the mix when you didn't know what was in it."

"I told you before that—"

"You leap first and look later. Not a good plan for staying alive. Come on. We'll wait for the police in the house." He stalked away, still managing to move silently despite his obvious anger.

"That wasn't what I was going to say, and I didn't leap first. I considered my options and decided that the best one didn't include letting you be killed while you slept," she threw back at him as she caught up.

"I wasn't asleep. I was out hunting a predator."

"Well, I would have known that if you'd bothered to inform me."

"You think I should have taken the time to give you a call before I went after the person heading for your apartment? Is that what you're saying?" They stepped into his house, and he flipped on a light, his movements sharp and filled with irritation.

"I—" The words caught in her throat as she took him in. Black hair hanging to his collar, faded jeans hugging lean hips, soft cotton shirt showcasing muscles in his chest and arms, ocean blue eyes shooting fire. He took her breath away, made every thought fly from her head.

She frowned, dropping the knife onto a granite island that separated the living area from a spacious kitchen. "Is this our first fight, Jonas, because if it is, I'd like to know. Make sure I get all the details of it right when I write about it in my diary."

He scowled, then shook his head, his lips twitching with a half smile. "You keep a diary?"

"No, but I'm thinking I might start. My life has gotten a lot more interesting in the past week."

"Too interesting. And, for the record, we've been fighting nonstop since we met."

"True, so how about we call a truce and admit that we both did what we had to."

"Too bad doing it didn't net us a bad guy. I'd have loved to ask a few questions." He opened the front door, stepping onto the porch as a police cruiser pulled in front of the house.

"You folks okay? We got a couple calls about an intruder," the deputy called, as he got out of the car, moved into the light from the open door so that they could see his face.

Dark hair and eyes, deep tan.

Marcus Williams.

"We're fine, but the guy who was here escaped," Jonas said, frustration still seeping through every word. Skylar understood. She felt it, too. One perp, that's all they needed to blow the case wide open.

Too bad this one had slipped through their fingers.

"Probably for the best. It's never a good idea for civilians to confront an intruder. Although, I guess neither of you are really that. How about we go inside, you tell me what you saw."

It didn't take long. Maybe a half hour. Another hour for Deputy Williams and another responding officer to sweep the grounds, search for evidence. There was nothing. Not even a footprint. Skylar wanted to be out on the field, tracking leads, trying to connect the dots so she could see the picture more clearly. Wanted to be anywhere but on Jonas's couch, sipping coffee and listening while the deputy told her what she already knew. No evidence. No clues. Nothing but their word that they'd seen someone stalking the house.

"Here's the thing, if you were anyone else, I'd say you saw a transient, but since you're you, I'm inclined to believe someone was here gunning for you. We've been running patrols every couple hours, but obviously missed the mark on this one. We'll increase our presence, but I can't guarantee it'll be enough. If you see someone again, stay in the house until backup arrives. You're going to the station to look at mug shots, right?"

"Right," Skylar answered, and Jonas frowned. Out of the loop and obviously not happy about it.

"I'll have your statements typed up when you get there. You can just add your John Hancock, and we'll be set. Call the station directly if there's any more trouble. We know the situation you're in better than 9-1-1, and we can mobilize and be here quickly." He handed Skylar a business card and she tucked it in her pocket.

"Thank you, Deputy." She walked onto the porch, but Jonas motioned her back.

"Let's not give a sniper a clear shot, okay?"

Next thing she knew, both men were out at the cruiser, and she was behind a closed door, twiddling her thumbs and waiting.

Again.

A minute passed. Two.

They were talking about the case, probably talking about her, and she was sitting on a couch letting them do it.

Not how she wanted to play things.

She was halfway to the door when it swung open, and Jonas walked in, his gaze sweeping her from head to toe. Braided hair and scuffed boots, soft sweater and faded jeans.

She blushed, heat sweeping up her face.

"You're flushed. Did you take your medicine?" He touched her forehead, and everything she'd felt the night before swept in.

She moved back.

"I'm fine. And, yes, I took it. Now, how about you stop worrying about me, and we get moving? Did Deputy Williams explain things?"

"Yes. It sounds like the guy whose bullet missed you by an inch paid for his mistake."

"That's what I was thinking."

"You think you'll recognize a mug shot of him?"

"I think so."

"Me, too."

"Good. Let's go." She grabbed the doorknob, but he tugged her back.

"Not so fast, Grady. We need to set up some ground rules, first. Starting with rule one. When I say 'stay down,' you stay."

"I've never been good at following rules."

"Get good, because I'm not willing to watch you die."

"Meaning?"

"I'll do whatever it takes to make sure you don't, and stupid moves on your part? They might not work out so well for either of us. I had a gun tonight. You didn't. I don't have a hit out on my head. You do. You should have thought of those things before you ran out into danger."

She had a biting retort on the tip of her tongue, almost let it fly, but there was something in Jonas's eyes, memories that still haunted him, regrets he'd never stop feeling. They stole her anger away.

"All right."

"That's it?" He frowned, pressed his palm to her forehead.

"Yes, and it's not the fever talking. You're right. I should have thought things through a little more. Needless risks aren't my style, but I'm not willing to watch you die any more than you are me. That influenced my decisions. Maybe more than it should have."

He eyed her for a moment, something hot flashing in his eyes, there and gone so quickly she wasn't sure she'd seen it.

"Good to know, Grady. Now come on. We've got work to

do, and a limited time to do it in." He stepped outside, and she followed.

She'd meant to handle the investigation alone. That's how she'd gone into it. No partner ever again. No chance of betrayal. But Jonas had stepped in, become what she didn't want and had told herself for years she didn't need.

He'd stepped in, and she wasn't going to ask him to step out. Didn't want him to step out.

Sometimes you have to risk everything to have something wonderful. That's what he'd said, and she thought that maybe he was right. Thought that maybe something wonderful was just waiting for her to reach out and take it. If she dared.

Did she?

Skylar wasn't sure, but as she climbed into the truck, waited for Jonas to climb in with her, she couldn't help wondering if she dared *not* reach for it.

Something wonderful?

Or the same thing she'd had for more years than she cared to think about?

Not much of a choice, but she was still afraid.

Afraid of having her heart filled and then having it emptied again.

Afraid.

But maybe not too afraid to try.

The thought filled her mind as Jonas pulled onto the highway and headed for the sheriff's department.

FOURTEEN

It took Jonas two seconds to choose the perp off a printed sheet that showcased twelve mug shots. Perp and victim. The guy had hung with the wrong crowd, and the crowd had turned on him. Maybe because he'd missed an opportunity to take out Skylar, or maybe because he'd only been a small piece of a very large picture.

Expendable and expended.

"That's him." He pointed to the third face in the second row, wondered if Skylar was pointing out the same one to the sheriff. The picture on the sheet showed a man who was gaunt, worn, with a vague look in hazy eyes. A drug addict or alcoholic. The guy had taken a wrong turn at some point in his life, and it had led to an open grave in the desert.

"You're sure?" Chief Deputy Mitchell asked, and Jonas nodded.

"It was too dark to see eye or hair color, but I got a good look at his bone structure, the shape of his nose and the angle of his jaw. It's him."

"Josiah Stanley, you really did it this time." Mitchell tapped the man's face with his finger, and shook his head.

"You've had dealings with him before?"

"Enough to know he was more interested in where he was

getting his next drink than having a lot of stuff. He committed crimes to feed the need for booze."

"You think he was a lackey, then?"

"Yeah. He had a reputation as a tracker an eon ago. Used to make some money taking people on desert excursions. Got drunk one too many times on the job, and that was that."

"So, someone might have hired him to find Skylar."

"That's my guess. It's hard to say, though, seeing as how he can't tell us the story." Mitchell steepled his fingers together, and eyed Jonas across the desk.

"I didn't kill him, if that's what you're thinking."

"I figured if you had, he'd have a bullet through the heart and his throat intact. What I'm wondering is if he knew who you were. If he did, he might have panicked, decided to cut his losses and take off on his own."

"I've never met the man." Jonas lifted the photo.

"People in the same industry keep tabs on each other, right? And when someone's really good at what he does, news of it travels. You were raised in the area, you came back to it, and not quietly. Most people in the community knew why you'd returned, what you'd been doing while you were gone. More than likely, Stanley knew, too." He shrugged. "Not that it matters. For whatever reason, he's dead."

"And we're no closer to answers than we were before you found his body."

"No, but two executions in a couple weeks...that's a big deal for our department. We're digging, and we're going to find out who is responsible."

But would they do it before another victim died?

The thought of Skylar lying in a shallow grave, her throat slit, a bullet in her head, had Jonas up and pacing across the room. "The hits were typical gang-style killings. What gangs are active in the area, Deputy?"

"What gangs aren't, is a better question. We get gangs

from New Mexico and California, and a few coming up across the border from Mexico. Much as I hate to say it, drugs are a big business in these parts."

"How about word on the street? Anyone taking credit for the killings?"

"It's quiet as a tomb. Our snitches say they haven't heard anything, and no one else seems to be talking."

"People don't talk when they're afraid. What are the main gangs? The big players?"

"You know, Sampson, I'm beginning to feel like I'm the one being interviewed here." Mitchell poured coffee from a carafe that sat on a corner of the desk. "Want some?"

"No. Thanks."

"In answer to your question, the bigger gangs are Phoenix based. The big players call the city home, and I doubt they'd put much effort into cutting down a small time player like Stanley."

"What about Redmond?"

"Now that's another question entirely. Redmond traveled a few times a month. Went away for a couple days and then came back. No one seems to know where he went. We're checking the contents of his house, trying to figure that out."

Someone knocked on the door and it opened.

Jonas felt Skylar's presence before she stepped in the room. Every nerve sprang to life, his body hummed, his palms itched to reach out, tug her to his side. Cheeks chapped from her week out in the sun, her hair pulled back into a tight braid, she crossed the room, dropped into a chair near the desk.

"Well, that was fun."

"Glad one of us enjoyed it." The sheriff followed her in, his steely gaze resting on Jonas. "I hear there was trouble out at your place this morning."

"That's right."

"And you still think your girlfriend should stick around?"

"I've told you seventeen *thousand* times, Sheriff, I am *not* his girlfriend, and I'm not leaving town."

"That's a lot of times to fit into…" Mitchell began as he glanced at his watch, not even trying to hide his amusement, "twenty minutes."

"It was a long twenty minutes," the sheriff responded, and Jonas wondered how many times he'd tried to insist Skylar leave town and how many times she'd refused. "But we do have a confirmed ID on the remains. How'd you do in here?"

"We got a match, too. Stanley was working with the posse that tried to take Skylar down." Mitchell handed the sheriff the photo.

"That's what I was afraid of." The sheriff raked a hand down his jaw, stared at the picture.

"Afraid of?" Jonas asked, and the sheriff met his eyes.

"I was hoping we had separate incidents. That maybe Redmond and Stanley's death didn't have anything to do with Skylar. She's a private investigator. She could have enemies she's unaware of."

"So, you wanted her to go home and take them with her?"

"I want this town to be safe, Sampson. However that happens, I'll be happy. I'd also have been happy to think Stanley and Redmond were taken out by a gang. That's simple and straightforward. The fact that Skylar came here looking for Redmond and found a boatload of trouble means we've got trouble in town. Trouble someone is working very hard to keep quiet."

"I was thinking the same, Sheriff," Mitchell spoke up. "Someone went to a lot of trouble to hide Redmond's body, then Skylar came to town and started asking around, insisting on answers. She stirred something up for sure."

"And if she'd died out in the desert, people would still be assuming she went out there sightseeing and got lost. Happens all the time, and whoever set up everything knew it. Take her out to the middle of nowhere. Make it look like she ran out of gas. Let the elements do the rest. With her out of the picture, Redmond's body might have been under that cement slab for centuries. I don't like it, and I want answers." The sheriff scowled and stood. "I need to get back to work. Call me if anything comes up."

He walked out, and Mitchell turned to Skylar. "He's right, you know."

"About me stirring up trouble?"

"About you leaving town. Whatever trouble we have here, there's a good chance it won't follow you home. Too much distance, too much effort and too much of a chance of being caught."

"I disagree. If this is gang related and drug related, there's plenty of money to throw around, and it's easy enough to throw it at a hit man." She touched the arrowhead that still hung from her neck, her fingers dancing along the turquoise beads to either side of it.

Long, strong fingers. Fingers that were as calloused as Jonas's, as capable. She could take care of herself, no doubt about that. But Jonas wanted to take care of her anyway. Wanted to bundle her up and ship her out to some place where she'd be safe. Too bad she wouldn't cooperate.

"To quote the sheriff, she's your girlfriend, do you think she should stick around? Or do you think maybe you can talk her into leaving town?" Mitchell shot Jonas a smile. He must have sensed what was in the air. The energy that pulsed between Skylar and Jonas when they were together.

"I'm not—"

"Don't ruin the moment, Grady."

"What moment?" she scowled.

"The moment when I acknowledge that you have a will of steel and tell Chief Deputy Mitchell that I'm not going to waste my breath trying to get you out of town." He pulled her to her feet, ignoring the heat that spread through him at the contact.

"So, I win?" She grinned, but he wasn't amused.

"No one wins, if you die."

"I'm not going to."

"From your lips to God's ear. Let's hope He's in a listening mood," Mitchell said as he led them outside.

"He always listens. He just doesn't always give us what we want," Skylar responded, her words twisting Jonas's gut, making him think of all that he'd wanted, of his fruitless prayers lifting up to the heavens.

Please, save my wife. My son.

Over and over and over again until the doctor had come to give him God's answer.

He'd prayed again as he and Skylar climbed the mesa, his fear pushing him back to a place of faith he hadn't been sure he'd ever return to.

The answer had been different, then.

Better.

But that didn't mean all his prayers would be answered the way he wanted them to be. It didn't mean assurance that the future would be bright and wonderful and free of trouble.

"What's wrong?" Skylar put a hand on his arm, as he got into the truck.

"Nothing."

"Something."

"Just thinking that you're right. God doesn't always give us what we want. Sometimes, that's for the best. Sometimes...I wonder."

"Yeah. Me, too. There's a bigger plan, I know that. Some huge tapestry that God is weaving, and I'm only a tiny part of it. He knows the colors and the patterns that work best, and He chooses carefully to make me fit. It's still hard, though, to accept the things that tear us up inside." She squeezed his hand as he started the truck, her rough palm pressed to his, pulling him back from the brink of all the memories that haunted him. Pulling him back to the moment, the woman, the gift that he was just beginning to believe God was giving him.

"I wish we had more to go on," she said, as he pulled away from the station, and he nodded.

"Me, too. The more answers we get, the more questions I have. You said Redmond worked at a local diner. How about we head over there and get some breakfast, see if anyone there has new information?"

"I'm not sure the sheriff would approve."

"When has disapproval ever stopped you?"

"Never." She laughed, and he imagined her in twenty years, laugh lines bracketing her mouth and fanning out from her eyes, age only adding to her beauty. Imagined himself beside her.

"Take the third left. It's about a half mile away. It surprised me that he worked so close to the sheriff's office, seeing as how he'd been shirking his obligation to pay child support for two years."

"A cop in Arizona isn't likely to know about a guy from New York who owes child support."

"I know, but it still surprised me that he'd risk it."

"Maybe he liked flaunting his ability to elude the authorities."

"That's the thing. He didn't change his identity, didn't go to any effort to hide. I'm not sure he thought of himself as eluding anything. The way his ex-wife put it, he had delusions of grandeur, and thought he was a whole lot more important than he was. I can't figure out why he wound up in a little town like Cave Creek, working as a line cook at a diner. He had two doctorates. He should have been able to get a job doing something else."

"He'd been kicked out of a university position for cheating. Most employers wouldn't look kindly on that."

"True, but, based on everything his ex said, I'd think Redmond would have gravitated toward big cities and more important jobs. Why here? That's what I keep wondering. If he had connections before he came to town, they might be the key to finding out who killed him. Here it is." She gestured to a fifties-style diner, its faded neon signs shouting that the place had the best burgers in town.

"Classy place," he said as he parked the truck.

"Exactly my point. A university professor with a big ego working here? It doesn't make sense."

"Let's go see what his coworkers have to say." Jonas got out of the truck, glancing around, checking for trouble. He didn't think there'd be an attack so close to the sheriff's office, but what he thought wouldn't matter if bullets flew and Skylar was hit.

"Are we in a race, Jonas? Because you're going to win. Your legs are a whole lot longer than mine," Skylar panted as they hurried to the door.

"Sorry. I want to limit our time out in the open as much as possible." He urged her inside, stepping in behind her, the scent of bacon and coffee filling his nose, mixing with the scent of Skylar.

"Howdy, folks. Getting an early start on your day, huh?" A skinny blonde sashayed toward them, her kohl-rimmed eyes settling on Skylar's face. "I know you, right?"

"I was in here a week ago, asking about Daniel Redmond."

"Thought so. Also, saw you on the news. Couldn't believe it when they found you alive out there. I had a friend once. Went out into the desert to take some pictures. Never came out."

"I'm sorry to hear that," Skylar offered, and the woman shrugged.

"He should have known better. He lived here his entire life. You? You're city. Guess you can be forgiven getting stuck out there."

"Thanks." Skylar's wry response didn't seem to register. The waitress continued to speak as she led them to a small booth near the kitchen.

"Me? I'd have a month's supply of water and food, plus a flare gun if I went out there. I won't. Don't much care for the desert even though I grew up here. Can I get you some coffee?" She tossed menus onto the table.

"Actually, I was hoping to speak with your manager."

"About Dan, right? We had cops in here all day, yesterday. Wouldn't tell us what it was about, but I have my suspicions."

"Do you?"

"Heard a body was pulled out of his backyard. My guess is it's him."

"Is there a reason why you think someone would murder him?"

"People either loved him or hated him. I guess someone might have hated him enough to do him in."

"Any idea who?"

"None. We didn't hang with the same crowd. Shelby might know, though. She owns the place. Probably spent more time with Dan than anyone else here."

"They dated?" Jonas asked, and the waitress laughed.

"Shelby date? She's married to the diner, and that's all she has time for. I just meant she worked more shifts with him. It's possible she saw who his friends were. She's in the back. I'll get her for you. How about I put in an order for two specials while I'm at it? Things can get crazy here when the before-church crowd arrives. Wouldn't want you to have to wait for your food."

"What's the special?"

"A three stack. Two eggs. Sausage. Pan fried potatoes."

"Sounds good to me."

"Two specials, then." She scribbled something on an order pad, and Skylar frowned again.

"One will be fine." Obviously, Skylar wasn't thrilled to have him order for her.

"Two. I'm hungry enough to eat both if you can't eat yours."

"Six pancakes, four eggs, sausage and potatoes? There is no way can you eat all that."

"Probably not, but I'm banking on you eating, so I'm not all that concerned about it. You're hungry, right?"

"Yes, but we don't have time to eat. Not a huge meal, anyway." Skylar tapped her fingers on the table, and the waitress huffed impatiently.

"No offense, but I have more prep to do before the rush. Want to make up your minds?"

"It's made. Bring two specials," Jonas said, because they needed to eat and because spending time where Redmond worked might give them some clue as to why he'd chosen to work there.

"I didn't expect this of you, Jonas." Skylar crossed her arms, her dark eyes shooting daggers.

"What?"

"The whole macho thing. You decide we eat, so we eat."

"Yeah, well, I didn't expect this of you, either."

"I'm not going to ask you what."

"Chicken."

"Fine. What didn't you expect?"

"That you'd be a sore loser. If sticking around to see if any of Redmond's associates showed up was your idea, you'd fight hard to stay all day and eat a dozen meals. Since it's mine, you're going to mope and call macho on me." He responded, and Skylar's lips quirked into a half smile.

"You know just how to play me, don't you, Jonas? Make me ask what I don't want to know, so you can drum some sense into my head. I'm sorry about the macho remark. I'm competitive. It's another thing I'm working on."

"It's also what kept you alive for six days, so I'm not complaining, but, just so we're clear, games aren't my thing. I'll never play them with you."

"Is that a promise?" Her smile fell away.

"Do you want it to be?"

She hesitated, then shrugged. "I don't like promises. No one ever keeps them. But maybe with you, things will be different. Right now, though, all I really want is to find some answers. I have the feeling time is running short, Jonas. It's making me antsy." She fiddled with the end of her braid, scooting back against the bench as the waitress returned with their order.

Honest, tough, funny, she was all those things.

And she was smart, her instincts good.

Her worry only added to his, and he dug into his breakfast, his mind racing ahead to the moment of confrontation when he would square off against Skylar's enemy.

It was coming, and he knew it.

Blood spurting over his hands, spilling onto the ground.

He shoved the memory away.

Not again.

He wouldn't let it happen again.

Please, God, help me keep it from happening again.

The prayer tripped out, as rough and raw as his emotions, and he didn't regret it. Faith had a way of clinging even when a person wanted to push it away. For once, he wasn't pushing.

FIFTEEN

She *was* hungry, and Jonas was right. Scoping out the diner, looking for Redmond's contemporaries, that made the meal doubly worthwhile.

Skylar dug into her second pancake, shoveling it in and swallowing it down so fast she barely had time to taste it. Starvation would do that to a person, and she'd been starved for almost a week, so hungry, she'd been physically sick with it. She'd lost at least a dozen pounds during her long hike. Her clothes were loose, her bones protruding. It was time to put some weight back on.

She forked up a sausage. Thought about inhaling it and following it up with a shot of maple syrup.

Then again, maybe she shouldn't be shoving food in her face with Jonas right across the table watching her with those blue-green eyes.

Staring at her with those blue-green eyes.

"What?" She dabbed a napkin to her mouth and took a sip of orange juice, trying to pretend she didn't want to eat every single bite of the food on her plate. Plus, anything left on his.

"Just admiring your ability to eat without chewing."

She laughed, nearly spewing juice across the table at him, coughing until he came around the table and patted her back.

"You okay?" His hand rested on her back, the heat of it spearing through her.

"Next time, wait until I swallow before you give me the unvarnished truth." She scooted away, and he smiled.

"You're nervous again."

"Nearly choking to death will do that to a person."

"No one chokes to death on juice."

"That's what everyone says until it happens."

He chuckled, moving back to his seat as the kitchen doors opened and a tall lean woman walked out.

"Morning, folks. I'm Shelby Hunter. Marcy said you wanted to speak with me." She was younger than Skylar expected. Maybe at the top edge of twenty, her hazel eyes oddly light against dark red lashes, short red hair spiking around her head.

"We were hoping you might be able to tell us a little bit about Daniel Redmond. I was in a week ago, but you were out of town."

"Skylar Grady, right?" She pulled over a chair, dropped into it, long legs stretched out, her arms crossed.

"That's right."

"There was a message from you on my desk when I got back to town, but by that time you were missing. Glad you're okay, and I'm glad we can finally connect. So, what is it you want to know about Dan?"

"I spoke with a manager while you were gone. He said Redmond worked here for several months. That he was a good employee. I wanted to confirm that."

"You spoke with Rick?"

"I think that was his name."

"Good manager. Knows his job, so whatever he told you, you can take it to the bank."

"I'd like your opinion, anyway."

"You and every cop in town." She smoothed her hair, and

it sprang up again. "Look, Redmond did his job. He showed up for work on time. He didn't cause trouble. In my opinion, that's a winning combination."

"Lots of people do their jobs and show up for work on time. That doesn't make them good employees," Jonas said, and Shelby turned her attention to him.

"You're Jonas Sampson, right? Saw a news story about you when I moved to town a few years back."

"That's a long time to remember a name." He frowned, and Skylar shot him a look she hoped would keep him from throwing out a bunch of questions that might close down the interview before it even began.

"I've got a good memory." She shrugged. "You're right, though, about Dan. All those qualities combined don't make a good employee, and I wouldn't say Dan was one. He did what he had to. Nothing more."

"You know a body was found behind his house, right?" Skylar tossed the line, hoping to reel in some information they could use.

"How could I not? Half of yesterday's customers told me about it."

"There's a good possibility the deceased is Redmond."

"I figured that, what with the police showing up at the diner. Look, I have a busy day ahead of me, and I don't have a lot of time to waste talking about a guy I barely knew. If you don't have anything else to ask, I need to go back to work."

"We want to know who murdered him, Shelby, and we were hoping you might have some idea."

"I really haven't given it much thought, but, the way I see it, you mess with the big dogs and you're going to get bit," she said as she stood, and Skylar's heart jumped.

"Big dogs?"

"I'll tell you what I told the police, and then I have to go.

Dan hung with a tough crowd. Not people I'd trust to have my back."

"Who?"

"You ever heard of the New Day Militia?"

"They have a compound twenty miles north of here, right?" Jonas asked, and Shelby nodded.

"That's right. They're big on independence, believe the government is out to get them. Redmond hooked up with a couple of brothers who are part of the group. Gerald and Mark Clovis. They used to come in here during off hours. Late at night. Really early in the morning. Any time they thought the dining room would be empty."

"Used to?"

"They got into an argument with another patron. Nearly came to blows. I asked them not to come back."

"Do you know where we can find the Clovis brothers?" Skylar pulled a paper napkin from the holder, fished a pen from her purse and got ready to write. This was the first she'd heard of Redmond's connection to a militia group, and she was ready to run with the information.

"Easiest way to find them is to go out to the compound, but I wouldn't recommend it. They're not nice people."

"Are they murderers?"

"They're bigoted rebels who believe they're a law unto themselves. Whether or not they're murderers, I couldn't say."

"But they *were* friends with Redmond?"

"If people like that can claim to have friends, then, yes. Now, if you'll excuse me. I need to finish prepping for the breakfast rush."

"Before you go, there's one more thing. The police found a body out in the desert last night."

"Good old Josiah Stanley. I saw it on the news. It's too bad. He was harmless enough."

"Did you ever see him hanging around with Redmond?"

"Hanging with Dan? I don't think—" She frowned. "Actually, now that I think about it, I did see them together once. I was heading home, and I saw Dan hanging around near the alley beside the diner. I thought he was alone, but then I realized Josiah was there. I figured maybe Dan was giving him something from the kitchen."

"Did you ask?"

"I didn't care enough to. Feeding one old man isn't going to break my business. Now I really do have to get back to work. Enjoy your meal. It's on the house." She walked away, not giving Skylar time to ask more questions.

That was fine.

She'd learned plenty.

And she planned to find out more.

She shoved her plate away and stood. "We need to go out to New Day."

"No." Jonas rose, too.

"What do you mean, 'no'?"

"Exactly what I said. We're not going out there."

"We just got the lead we've been searching for. Are you telling me that we shouldn't follow up on it?"

"I'm telling you that we're not the police. We don't have their authority, or their manpower. If what Shelby said is right, heading to the compound without either of those things would be foolish."

"So, we're just supposed to sit around hoping the police are doing their jobs?"

"We're supposed to make sure the police have all the information we do, and we will. Shelby said herself that she told the police about the connection between Redmond and the Clovis brothers. Mitchell is a good cop, and he's thorough. There's no doubt in my mind, if he already has the information, he's following up on it."

"*Mitchell* is a good cop? You're not including the sheriff in that?"

"No, because I'm not sure what the sheriff's priorities are. After Deputy Williams's comment about it being an election year, I'm wondering how focused the sheriff is on the case. Come on. Let's get out of here. We'll call Mitchell on the way back to my place and tell him about the connection to Josiah Stanley. Didn't seem like Shelby told the police about that. We'll see what he has to say."

"If Shelby knew about Redmond's connections to New Day, other people must have. It's strange that no one mentioned it to me before now."

"Fear is a powerful enemy. New Day has been around for a few decades, and they've earned a reputation for brutal retaliation against anyone who crosses them. Several members have been accused of murder. No one has ever been convicted." Jonas pulled onto the road and tossed his cell phone into Skylar's lap. "Go ahead and call Mitchell."

She did, leaving a message on his voice mail, her mind spinning with possibilities. "They've been accused of murder, so it's possible they've committed it. That makes it even more likely they were involved in Redmond's death."

"Maybe."

"I still think we should pay them a visit."

"Even if we did, which we *won't,* it's unlikely we'd make it onto the compound. The group is closed to the public. They exist under the guise of a religious sect that abhors the trappings of modern life."

"Like the Amish?"

"Hardly. They're preparing the way for a new messiah, and they say he's going to be born into their numbers. They control everything that comes in with the express purpose of keeping what they call the new order from being tainted. At least, that's what their followers are told."

"You know a lot about the group, Jonas."

"I should. One of my jobs as border patrol agent was to keep illegal firearms from being brought into the country. We suspected that New Day was one of the prime destinations for anything that made it through, but we weren't able to prove it."

"It's hard to believe a group like that doesn't get more press."

"They've had their share, but only locally. Their prime objective is to overthrow the government, but they aren't advertising that. Staying under the radar by working within the law is how they've kept going for so long. The crimes they do commit, they commit secretly. In other words, they pay their taxes and their bills, they act civil and don't cause problems."

"That matches what happened to Redmond. His body being buried where it would never have been found if I hadn't started them looking, then the accidental way I was supposed to die. Commit the crime, but make sure to keep it hidden."

"Exactly. Just because the group hasn't been convicted of crimes doesn't mean they haven't committed plenty of them. The more they commit, the more likely it is they'll get caught. If I remember correctly, at least a few of the members have been arrested. None of the charges have stuck, but there's always a first time."

"Let's hope this is it."

"Hoping is great, but we're not going to try to take them down ourselves." He pulled up in front of his house, reaching over and rubbing a thumb along the corner of her mouth. "Maple syrup."

"What?" She blinked, tried to focus, but every thought was gone, wiped away by one gentle touch of his thumb.

"You have maple syrup on your face."

"Oh." She reached up and rubbed the spot, trying to rub away the heat that was turning her insides to mush.

Not possible, though.

Not possible to move, either, as he leaned forward, his lips brushing hers, settling there. And she was lost again, her dreams welling up and filling her heart until she had to break away.

She reached for the door, blindly opening it and jumping out.

"Sky, wait!" Jonas got out of the truck and grabbed her arm, pulling her to a stop at the threshold of the apartment.

He nudged her into the house, closed the door, crowding her into the tiny living room and taking up more than his fair share of space.

It should have bothered her that he seemed to steal her thoughts and her breath without effort. That having him close made her forget all the reasons why she shouldn't take chances with her heart.

Should have bothered her, but it didn't.

Because it was Jonas doing those things, and she thought that maybe he needed her around just as much as she needed him. His loss, his guilt, his need to protect his heart were all things she understood. She looked into his eyes, studied his face, her heart opening in a way it hadn't in a very long time.

"If you're going to apologize, don't. The kiss was a mutual thing, and I'm not sorry for it. I just…need some space."

"Good to know, but I wasn't going to apologize."

"Then, what is it?"

"Sunday."

"What?"

"It's Sunday. I thought you might like to come to church with me."

"I'm not sure I have anything to wear. I didn't think I'd

be in town for more than a couple of days, so I didn't plan for Sunday service."

"You look perfect in what you're wearing."

"Jeans and a T-shirt?"

"You'd look good in a gunnysack, Grady. I'll be ready in thirty. Keep the door locked and the alarm set until I knock," he said, walking out before she could offer more excuses.

And maybe she didn't need more.

Because it was Jonas she was going to church with. Aside from God, she'd never believed in much, but she did believe in him.

It wasn't forever.

But it was a start.

SIXTEEN

She should have said no.

Skylar scowled at the small pile of clothes on the bed. Jeans and T-shirts. Mostly faded and worn. One pair of black slacks, black heels and a square-necked sweater that she hated because it showed too many scars and she had only packed it because it happened to be clean.

A motley assortment.

She couldn't go to church wearing any of it.

Not that God cared. She knew He didn't. He met people where they were, how they were, but Skylar had spent too many years going to church in holey clothes and broken shoes to want to wear anything but her best when she attended. Too caught up in their addictions to care, her parents hadn't even made Skylar or Tessa brush their hair or wash their faces before they left the house. It had been Mrs. Peach who had taught them to take care of their appearances and who had brought them to church, insisting she needed an escort to walk her there.

Mrs. Peach.

The name was enough to make Skylar smile.

Widowed and lonely and looking for someone to pour herself into, the elderly woman had taken on the task of raising two little girls who were raising themselves. She'd been

Skylar's safety net until she'd passed away. And she'd been Skylar's first taste of loss. In memory of her friend, Skylar had trudged to church by herself from the time she was ten and Tessa had quit going until she'd finally escaped the mean little neighborhood she'd grown up in.

Mrs. Peach would be happy to know Skylar had found faith in the run-down church they'd attended together.

She wouldn't be pleased that Skylar was standing over a perfectly good pile of clothes bemoaning her limited choices.

She frowned, grabbing the slacks and sweater, throwing them on and shoving her feet into the heels.

"Be honest with yourself, Sky. You're more worried about what Jonas will think of your outfit than you are about wearing it to church," she muttered as she stared in the mirror, hitched up her sweater to cover the scars a little more, loosened her hair and let it fall around her shoulders. Too many curls, but there wasn't much she could do about them, so she let them be. Slicked on gloss and a little mascara. Frowned at her reflection again.

A soft knock sounded on the door, and her time was up.

She grabbed her Bible, hurried into the living room as the door opened and Jonas walked in, punched in the alarm code and smiled.

He made slacks and a button-up shirt look good, his dark hair brushed back from his face, his eyes burning with interest as they followed Skylar across the room.

"You clean up good, Grady."

"So do you." He smelled good, too. Soap and aftershave and something indefinable and masculine.

"Looks like you have more than one scar to show for your partner's betrayal." His finger touched the purple circle beside her collarbone, and she shivered.

"Like I said, I was shot three times. Twice in the chest. Once in the stomach."

"I wish your partner was still alive, so I could have a... chat with him." The coldness in his words, the anger in his gaze left no doubt about how serious he was.

"Then I'm glad he's not. I wouldn't want you to go to prison for beating up pond scum." She offered a shaky smile. Unsure. Sure. All the things she wanted wrapped up in the hope that she could make this thing that had never worked before work; make this idea, this dream of a real family she'd had since she was a little girl listening to her parents scream obscenities at one another, become a reality.

It was a big risk, and she still wasn't sure she should be taking it.

"You look sad." His traced a path from the scar to her jaw, tilting her head, looking down into her eyes.

"I just don't want to put too much hope in this, Jonas. I don't want to start believing in it, and then find out it was just a moment in time, a blip on the radar. I want more than that."

"If by *this* you mean us, then you can stop worrying. We're not just a moment or a blip. I don't know where we're heading, but I'm not going anywhere until we find out."

"Isn't that what every guy says when a new couple is starting out?"

"Then you admit we're a couple? I thought it would take you at least another day to get to that point." He chucked her under the chin, opened the door. "Come on. We need to get moving or we'll be late. I don't want to have to explain why to Debby."

"I thought you said she was one of the most understanding people you'd ever met."

"She's also one of the biggest tyrants."

"I don't believe you. She seemed sweet as pie when we met."

"She's sweet, all right. Until you cross her, then, she's a

tyrant. I know this for fact since I crossed her more than one time when I was a teen." He smiled and led her to the truck, opening the door and waiting for her to get in.

It took less than ten minutes to drive to the church Jonas attended. Modest and small, it boasted a filled-to-overflowing parking lot and one too many sets of eyes watching as Jonas and Skylar made their way across it.

"People are staring," she whispered as they approached the front door.

"You're a beautiful woman, so why wouldn't they?"

"That's not it, and you know it."

"Maybe they're just surprised to see me with someone. More than one of them has tried to set me up on a date."

"So, you're the eligible bachelor of the congregation?"

"I was. Your visit should change my status." He pressed his hand to her lower back, urging her into the sanctuary.

"Hidden motives, Jonas?"

"My only motive is you." His words shivered through her as they walked down the center aisle.

Gleaming wood floors and old stained-glass windows added beauty to what might have been a plain building. Several dozen people sat in the pews, their eyes tracking Skylar and Jonas as they made their way to the front.

"Jonas! Skylar! I'm so glad you could make it." Debby waved from the front pew, her face glowing with excitement as she gestured for them to join her.

"I'm here every week, Debby, so I'm assuming it's not me you're excited about seeing." Jonas dropped a kiss on her cheek and offered his father a brief nod.

"I'm always excited to see you, but I have to admit, having a celebrity sitting in our pew is doing wonders for my reputation. Every lady in my Bible study is going to be begging to hear all the details of your experience. No worries, though, I'll remind them that it's your business to share."

"And act like she shared it all with you?" Richard asked, and she smiled.

"Of course. Come sit beside me, Skylar. Tell me how you're doing."

"A lot better than I was the last time we met."

"Are you finding everything you need at Rayne's place?"

"Yes. I really appreciate her letting me stay there."

"Rayne is a wonderful person. Though, I suppose I'm biased since I'm her mother."

"You're not biased. She *is* wonderful. Will she be here today?"

"She goes to a larger church in Phoenix. This is the one she grew up in, but kids need to branch out when they get older, put some distance between themselves and their parents. I'm sure you were the same way."

Skylar nodded, though she hadn't really had much of a choice. Her father died a month before she graduated high school. Even before he'd died, she'd been independent. She'd had to be.

"She should be over at our place for lunch this afternoon. Will you be there?"

"I—"

"We talked about this before, Debby. It's not safe," Jonas cut in, and Skylar was glad she hadn't been left to answer. She probably would have agreed without thinking about the consequences.

"We have a security alarm, and I have a rifle, but I doubt I'll need it. It's Sunday afternoon. No one is going to commit murder on the Lord's Day," Richard said, and Jonas snorted.

"You don't really believe that, Dad."

"Maybe not, but I don't see how Skylar is any safer at your place than she will be at ours."

"She isn't, but that doesn't mean I want you exposed to the danger she's in."

"What we're exposed to should be our choice, and Deb and I both agreed that—"

"Rich, let it drop." Debby put a hand on her husband's arm, stopping any further discussion.

"Right. You're right. Sorry." He offered a tight smile and turned his attention toward the front of the church. Obviously, there was a lot of baggage between father and son, but it seemed both were trying to build a strong relationship. Skylar would have given so much to have that opportunity with her parents.

"Penny for your thoughts," Jonas whispered as the strains of the first hymn filled the sanctuary.

"I was just thinking how nice it would be to have lunch invitations and arguments and…parents."

"It is nice. Even when it drives me crazy." He patted her knee, the gesture light and easy, drawing her into the family, letting her know she belonged.

Funny how quickly he'd done that.

In the two years she'd dated Matthew, she'd visited his family three times, always at formal occasions. A wedding, an engagement party, a New Year's bash. He'd mingled with the crowd of relatives, keeping Skylar at his side but never really including her. She'd felt as out of place as she had in her childhood home.

Here, sitting between Jonas and Debby, she felt absorbed into the family, accepted by the tight-knit group.

She glanced at Jonas as they stood for the second hymn, and he met her eyes, smiled that easy smile of his, and her heart jumped, her stomach fluttered.

Sitting in the church, her arm pressed to Jonas's as the pastor spoke, she could almost believe that what they were creating would last.

Love didn't have to be complicated. It didn't have to be the high highs and low lows of her parents' relationship, or the daily phone calls, the constant vying for attention that her relationship with Matthew had demanded, the needy, grasping love he'd showered on her.

It could just...*be.*

Two people, enjoying each other's company. Enjoying each other. Two people working together toward a common goal.

Two people who were meant to be.

For whatever reason.

Just be.

Together.

The pastor finished speaking, and Skylar stood for the final hymn, her heart thudding as she bowed her head for the benediction.

"No matter where you go this week, no matter how dark the circumstances of your life seem to be, God is with you. He will not abandon you, will not turn away from you. It is His strength that will see you through." The pastor's words filled the sanctuary, sank into Skylar's soul.

His strength.

Not hers.

She'd do well to remember that in the next few days. Otherwise, she might do what she shouldn't, take the information Shelby had given her and run with it.

"Ready?" Jonas asked, his warm breath tickling her hair, her heart leaping in response.

"Of course," she said and meant it.

"Are you two going back to your place?" Debby asked as they stepped outside.

"Yes," Jonas answered.

"No," Skylar responded at the same time, and Skylar frowned.

"I thought we'd head over to the sheriff's office. I want

to check in with Mitchell, see if he got my message," Skylar explained.

"Calling would be easier," Jonas suggested.

"I'd also like to speak with the sheriff. I want to find out if he knew about Redmond's connection to New Day before I got to town," Skylar continued.

"If you need a car to get there, I have an extra one you can borrow," Richard offered.

"Don't help, Dad," Jonas muttered, and Skylar smiled.

"I wouldn't want to put you out, Mr. Sampson."

"You're not. I have an old station wagon sitting in my garage. Nothing fancy, but it runs. You're welcome to it if you want," Richard said.

"That's generous of you, but—"

"Just smile and say thank you, dear. We'll drop it off at Jonas's house later today." Debby patted her hand, tugged Richard away.

"Together, those two are like a runaway train," Jonas said as he climbed into the truck.

"Maybe, but I like them."

"Me, too, but I don't want you driving around in their station wagon alone. Just so we're clear on that."

"Does that mean you're going to drive me to the sheriff's office?"

"Is that blackmail I'm hearing, Grady? I take you or you go on your own?"

"Blackmail is such an ugly word. Let's call it a friendly little bribe. You take me, and I won't drive the station wagon there."

"Sweeten the pot, and I might agree."

"You drive me, and I won't drive the station wagon *or* visit New Day?"

"So, you're still thinking about that, huh?"

"Thinking about it, but I know when to back off. This is one of those times. Whether I like it or not."

"Good, and since that's off the table, we're back to you sweetening the pot."

"How about a meal?"

"You can cook?"

"Only if it's from a box, but I do buy a mean pizza."

"Is dessert included in that?"

"Cookies? It's the one dessert I know how to bake myself."

"I can't resist a homemade cookie, so I guess you've got yourself a deal. Let's go visit Mitchell and the sheriff. You can buy me that meal after this is all over and the bad guys are behind bars. But, for the record, I would have taken you to the sheriff's office without a bribe."

"For the record, I know."

He laughed, pulling onto the highway. "Once we're through there, I want to go back to my place and do some more research on the Clovis brothers. The name is familiar, and I'm thinking I might have read it in connection to a criminal case that was in the paper a couple years ago. One of the brothers was arrested, maybe both, but I don't remember what for."

"Murder?"

"That would make things easy, wouldn't it? But I think it was something more mundane. Weapons or trafficking."

"I—"

"Do you have your seat belt on?"

"Yes. Why?" Surprised, she looked down, double checking.

"It looks like company is coming."

"Where?" Skylar shifted in her seat, trying to see out the back window. The road was dotted with vehicles.

A black sedan.

A red sports car.

A few jeeps.

An eighteen-wheeler.

So many vehicles surrounded them that, for a moment, Skylar didn't see the danger coming.

When she did, she couldn't look away.

Large and bulky, an oversize SUV barreled through traffic, weaving its way from one lane to another.

"He's coming fast."

"Hang on. I'm going to try to outrun him."

"Outrun him? Are you nuts? This truck is a hundred years old!"

"Don't dis the truck, Grady," Jonas growled, pulling past a slower moving vehicle.

"We don't have the horsepower to outrun them. We need another plan."

Fast.

Because the SUV was closing in.

"Call for backup and hang on. I'm going to jump the median."

But it was too late.

The SUV kissed their bumper, and Skylar braced for impact as she punched numbers into her cell phone. Prayed she was hitting the right ones.

Come on.

Come on.

The phone rang. Once. Then, again.

Jonas shouted something, but Skylar could barely hear past her thundering pulse. A 9-1-1 operator picked up as the SUV slammed the back of the truck.

Skylar screamed, the phone dropping from her fingers.

"Hold on!" Jonas swerved to the left, bouncing into the median and braking hard, the SUV speeding past them. Stopping.

"They're getting out!"

Young guy. Short blond hair.

Handgun pointed straight at Skylar's head.

She dived for cover as glass shattered, exploding into the truck, showering down on her.

"Stay here." Jonas opened the glove compartment, pulled out a pistol.

"No! It's too dangerous." She shouted the protest, but he was already opening the door, firing.

An engine roared.

Jonas edged out from behind the cover of the door.

And silence fell as quickly as chaos had descended.

Skylar straightened, grabbing the phone, giving the operator their location and getting out of the truck, her legs so shaky she didn't know if they'd hold her weight.

"Get back in the truck, Grady." Jonas strode toward her, blood dripping from a cut on his cheek, staining his white shirt.

"You're hurt."

"A scratch."

"Scratches don't bleed like that." She pulled him to the truck, shoved him into the driver's seat.

"We don't have time for this. The perp is getting away while you're poking at my face."

"I'm not poking, I'm looking. You're going to need stitches." She took off her jacket, pressed the sleeve against the three-inch gash.

"It's fine." He tried to push her hand away.

"No, it's not. Now let me take care of it."

"I can take care of it myself, Grady."

"So, it's okay for you to take care of me, but not the other way around?"

"I never said that."

"Then stop fighting me, and let me see if I can get the bleeding to stop."

He scowled but didn't protest again.

"Did you see a license plate?" Skylar hadn't seen much of anything. Just the color of the vehicle, the make. Dodge SUV. Black. Newish.

"It didn't have one, but I did get a good look at the driver, the gunman and the vehicle. Hopefully, that will help the police track them down quickly."

Sirens filled the air as the sheriff's car pulled up behind them, but Skylar kept applying pressure to the wound, kept imagining something worse than glass striking Jonas's cheek. A bullet piercing his flesh, taking his life.

She shuddered, and Jonas hooked an arm around her waist, tugged her into the space between his knees.

"It's okay, Grady. I'm fine."

"But what if you weren't?"

"I am. That's all that counts. Come on. Let's go see what the sheriff has to say." He took the jacket from her hand, pressed it to his cheek and stood.

"He's going to say what he always says. I need to go home. And I'm going to say what I always do. *No.*"

But she followed Jonas anyway, across a dozen feet of median to the sheriff's idling vehicle.

SEVENTEEN

Fifteen stitches weren't too bad compared to being dead.

Jonas thought about telling his stepmother and sister that. Both hovered by his side, offering water and pain meds and all manner of comfort foods.

He didn't want any of it.

What he wanted was to find Skylar.

She'd hung out at the hospital while the E.R. doctor stitched him up, driven him back home, stood at the edge of the entourage of people who'd heard about Jonas's injury and come to visit. He'd felt the weight of her stare, knew she was there even when he couldn't see her.

Her presence was that strong, his awareness of her that compelling.

And now she was gone.

He frowned, glancing around the living room. "Where's Skylar?"

"She and Dad went over to the apartment. She had to make a few phone calls and didn't want to be intrusive."

"I take it those were her exact words." Jonas stood, brushing off Debby's concern as he walked to the door.

"Yes. But I have a feeling you're not worried about being intrusive, and I have a feeling you're going to head right over there to see what she's up to." Rayne smirked as he opened the door, strode out into bright sunlight.

He ignored the words and the smirk.

He always did what he had to, and what he had to do right then was make sure that Skylar was exactly where she was supposed to be. The gunman who'd run them off the road had meant business. It was only by the grace of God that Skylar hadn't been injured.

Or worse.

Just the thought filled him with fury.

He'd seen her scars. He knew what she had been through.

She wouldn't go through it again.

He'd make sure of it.

"Mom said you and Skylar sat next to each other at church today." Rayne followed him across the yard.

"That's right."

"She said you looked real chummy. She even said Skylar makes you smile and since even I can barely do that, I figure that says a lot about your feelings for her."

"I'm assuming there's a point to this, sis?"

"Just that Skylar is exactly the kind of woman you need in your life, and I hope you're not going to mess up your chances with her."

"Thanks for the vote of confidence."

"I didn't mean that the way it sounded. It's just that you always overthink things, always try to plan everything so there aren't any variables and no surprises. Real life is filled with spontaneous opportunities. When they come, we need to grab them with both hands and hold on tight."

"What makes you think I'm not already doing that?" He stopped at the top of the steps, turning to face Rayne. She looked tired, dark shadows beneath her eyes, her face pale.

His little sister.

Grown up.

Living her own life.

Maybe even keeping her own secrets.

"I think it, because you loved Gabriella. Because you blame yourself for her death, for your baby's death. Because, maybe somewhere in that warped brain of yours, you've decided that you don't deserve another shot at happiness."

"Whether I deserve it or not, it's been handed to me. I'd be an idiot not to take it."

"I'm glad we agree. Now go in there and get your girl. Otherwise, you'll have to spend the rest of your life regretting that you didn't. That kind of regret isn't the kind I'd wish on my worst enemy, and it's definitely not something I'd wish on my favorite big brother." She smiled, but there was something in her eyes. Sadness? Fear?

"I'm your *only* big brother." He ruffled her hair, looked into her eyes. The sadness was still there, changing her from carefree college student into burdened adult.

"What's wrong, Rayne?"

"Nothing a good night's sleep won't fix. I'm beyond exhausted. This thesis is kicking my butt. I can't wait to get it finished." She wasn't telling him the whole truth, the words brittle and tight.

"I'm your big brother. I know you, and I know there's more than a thesis weighing on your mind. Spill it."

"You have enough on your plate, right now. I'm not going to add more to it by telling you my tales of woe. Go find Skylar. I'm going to take a nap. We'll talk when both of us have more time."

"I always have time for you, you know that, right?"

"Of course, but I'm still going to take a nap." Her smile was more genuine this time, her eyes less haunted, and she walked away, her blond hair swinging as she jogged down the stairs and back to the house.

He'd need to keep an eye on her. Make sure she wasn't

burning the candle at both ends, working herself too hard. Make sure there wasn't a guy standing in the wings somewhere, pushing her buttons and making her miserable. Rayne had a need to please and a strong desire to help and heal. It's why she'd decided to become a social worker. But the same need that made her good at her job also made her vulnerable, her need to help and heal attracting men who took advantage of both those things.

Men like the scum Skylar had been engaged to.

He frowned, not liking the thought.

His baby sister deserved a lot better than that.

Skylar deserved better.

He hoped he could give it to her.

He stepped into the apartment, greeted his father, scanning the otherwise empty room. "Where's Skylar?"

"She left about twenty minutes ago. The sheriff called and asked her to come in and look at mug shots. He has a lead on the guy who shot out the window of the truck."

"She's gone?" He hoped he'd heard wrong.

Really hoped he'd heard wrong.

Skylar out on her own with an armed gunman hunting her wasn't something he wanted to think about.

"The sheriff was pretty insistent that she go, so I let her borrow my car. Rayne can give me and Deb a ride home if Skylar isn't back before we're ready to leave."

"Please, tell me you're kidding, Dad. Tell me you didn't hand car keys to a woman who has half the state of Arizona gunning for her." His voice rose, and he took a deep breath, tried to calm down.

"You're exaggerating, son. Even if you weren't, Skylar is a grown woman with a good head on her shoulders. She's a former police officer, a current private detective. She survived a week lost in the Sonoran and a couple days hanging out with you. She's tough as nails. She asked for the keys. I said yes. Seemed like a no-brainer to me."

"Someone is trying to kill her. No-brainer or not, you should have told her to wait."

"For you?"

"For *someone*. Me. A police escort. Anyone with a gun who might actually be able to protect her if she gets into trouble."

"She'll protect herself. That's the kind of woman she is."

"Would you say that if she were Debby or Rayne?"

Richard's lips tightened, and he shook his head. "No, but the closest Deb has ever gotten to defending herself is swinging a fly swatter at a wasp. Your sister wouldn't know the barrel of a gun if it jumped up and hit her in the face. Neither of them has the experience or training Skylar does."

"That's not the point."

"The point is, your heart is working overtime, and your head has gone to lunch." Richard grabbed a sheaf of papers, thrust it at Jonas.

"What's this?"

"Skylar asked me to do some research before she left. Wanted some information on New Day. I have half a dozen articles about the organization. Three about the Clovis brothers. Seems like they've run into the law a time or two. Never ended up in jail, though."

"Thanks, Dad. I'll look at everything later. Right now I need to go find Skylar."

"You just had fifteen stitches put in your face. I'm not sure going out is a good idea."

"Fortunately, stitches in my face won't affect my gun arm or my aim. I'll be fine."

"Take the articles with you, then. Skylar wanted them ASAP."

"Right." He'd give her the articles, and he'd give her a piece of his mind.

Or two.

The rope incident on the mesa had been foolish. Going out alone a few hours after nearly being killed? That was even worse.

His cell phone rang as he shoved the rolled articles into his jacket pocket.

"Hello?"

"Jonas? It's Skylar." Her voice sent a wave of relief through him, and he bit back the angry words that threatened to roll of his tongue.

Keep your cool, Sampson.

Be reasonable.

"Where are you?"

"Sitting in the sheriff's office, waiting for him to bring in some mug shots he wants me to look at."

"You *should* be sitting in my sister's apartment waiting for me to give you a ride."

"Probably, but I got caught up in the moment. The sheriff thinks he knows the identity of the men we saw today. Said he had some mug shots for me to look at. I couldn't resist coming in to see them."

"Not even long enough to find a safer way to get there? I was a hundred yards away, Skylar. Didn't it occur to you to ask for an escort?"

"It did, but—"

"What?"

"What happened today scared me. I can't lose you, Jonas. You've come to mean too much to me."

"And you don't think I feel the same way?"

"I know you do, I just…seeing you bleeding like that, knowing it was my fault. It got to me."

She didn't need to explain.

He understood every feeling she'd had as she'd pressed her jacket to his cheek. Only his wound had been minor. The one *he'd* pressed his hands to had not been.

Blood-stained hands.

Endless guilt.

Yeah. He understood.

"I get it, Skylar. I don't like it, but I get it."

"Thanks. Listen, I asked your father to search online for a few key phrases while I was gone. I would have called him, but I don't have the number to your sister's apartment. I had to get this number from Chief Deputy Mitchell. Would you mind giving it to me so I can check in and see if he came up with anything?"

"No need for the number, I'm in the apartment and I have the articles. I'll bring them when I pick you up."

"Your dad works quick. Did he find anything interesting?" She ignored his comment about picking her up. It was probably for the best.

She'd protest.

He'd insist.

They'd do the same dance they'd been doing since they met, and, this time, Jonas planned to lead.

"I haven't had a chance to read through the articles, yet, but he says the Clovis brothers are in a few of them. They've had run-ins with the police, but they haven't done any time."

"What kind of run-ins? Do the articles say?"

"Hold on." He scanned the printed sheets his father had marked with the brothers' name, frowning as he read the information in the first article. "Looks like both were arrested a year ago on charges that they'd stolen artifacts from Native American burial sites. They were released a couple days later. Lack of evidence is what the article says. Funny, I don't remember reading about this."

"I guess it wasn't big news."

"I guess not." He scanned the second article. "Okay. The older brother was also arrested three years ago. Want to guess what he was suspected of?"

"Trafficking in stolen Native American artifacts?"

"Exactly. Same deal. Arrested. Released a few days later. Not enough evidence to hold him. Looks like a pattern."

"You said there were several articles. Were there more arrests?"

"Three articles on the brothers. No more arrests. The third article was in the paper six months ago. I remember reading it. The author is a friend of mine, a Navajo who was investigating the theft of sacred tribal objects. The Navajo Nation was demanding restitution from those they thought were responsible, but the sheriff's office said there wasn't enough proof to make anyone pay. My friend wrote a pretty scathing commentary in the Sunday paper."

"Were the Clovis brothers mentioned in it?"

"Not that I recall." He looked down as his father pointed to a paragraph near the bottom of the page. "Actually, they *are* in it. Just a brief mention about their criminal pasts and arrests."

"Interesting. Redmond had doctorates in archeology and ancient studies. He knew plenty about the native peoples of North America. Probably enough to identify and value artifacts. Shelby said he and the Clovis brothers were tight. The brothers might be able to handle the actual thefts, but I bet they'd be hard pressed to tell the difference between modern artifacts and antique ones. They'd have needed someone who could do that for them. Someone who could appraise their cache, make sure they got a fair price for it on the black market. We were looking for a connection, Jonas. I think we've found it."

"It makes sense. An organization like New Day doesn't run on stupidity. They'd have known they needed an expert if they were going to make top dollar, and Redmond had a reputation for being an expert and a cheat. If they put out feelers, asked around, his name would have popped up."

"And, if approached with an opportunity for quick cash, I doubt Redmond would have refused it. Even if he had to get a job at the diner to cover his real reason for being in town. Once I'm done here, I think we should—"

A voice rumbled in the background, cutting off Skylar's words.

"The sheriff is here. I've got to go. See you in an hour or so, okay?"

"I'll come pick you—"

But she'd already hung up, and Jonas did the same, scowling as he shoved the phone into his pocket and met his father's eyes. "Thanks for the research, Dad. Because of it, we're finally heading in the right direction."

"No thanks necessary. I may be a boring cartographer, but that doesn't mean I don't love a good puzzle."

"Who says being a cartographer is boring?"

"You. About a thousand times when you were living at home."

"I was a dumb kid, and I didn't realize how good I had it. I need to get out of here. Give Deb a kiss for me, and keep an eye on Rayne. She's looking tired."

"I guess you're heading to the sheriff's office?"

"You guess right."

"Be careful, okay? I know you're a tough guy, and I know you can take care of yourself, but you're my son, so I reserve the right to worry about you."

"I'll be careful." He glanced at the articles again, frowning. "Do you remember reading any of these before today?"

"Sure. The one that got me the most riled up was the one written by your buddy. Thousands of artifacts stolen. Tens of thousands of dollars gone. Not to mention the historical value for the tribe. A priceless, irreplaceable collection. All of it vanished, and no one seems willing to do anything about it." He shook his head.

"Who could? There hasn't been enough evidence to throw the book at anyone."

"Maybe not, but some of the students in my topography class at the university are citizens of the Navajo Nation. We've talked about the stolen artifacts a few times. They blame the sheriff. Say he's not doing his job, not working hard enough to close the cases. It surprised me to hear it, because the crime rate around here is lower than it's been in years. That's got to say something about Smithson's work ethic," Jonas's father responded, walking to the refrigerator and pulling out a soda.

"Either that, or it says something about his team of deputies. I'll see you later." Jonas stepped outside, the cold evening air slicing through his shirt.

The sun had fallen below distant mountains, trailing vivid purple clouds in its wake. Dusk had a feel and weight, the silence of it reminding Jonas of the nights he'd spent chasing trails through a lonely wilderness. He'd loved the expanse of the sky sprinkled with stars. Loved the way the silence of the evening gave way to the melody of the night. Frogs and birds of prey. Coyote and mountain lion. They were part of it all, and he'd been part of it, too. One with nature, the way Pops had taught him to be.

One with himself.

At peace with God, the stunning beauty of creation bringing him closer than he had ever been to understanding the power and glory of the Creator.

He'd let the gang take that from him.

Let them win, just as Skylar had said.

But their victory didn't have to be permanent.

He'd been knocked down for the count but not down forever.

Jonas Sampson the contractor was about to retire.

The Shadow Wolf was about to return.

The hunter. The tracker. The man who knew exactly where he belonged.

That's the direction he'd been heading since the day he'd agreed to search for Skylar. The yes after dozens of nos. A shift in perspective that he'd only noticed when he was deep into the mission, searching for answers, working with someone as driven and committed to justice as he was.

God's plan.

As much as he'd tried to fight it, Jonas couldn't deny the truth. Now, with one mission nearly complete, he was ready to move onto another and another, ready to go where God led, use the gifts he'd been given, seek justice over and over again.

His future lay in that direction.

And it lay with Skylar.

Rayne was right. No more caution. No more "wait and see." He'd found someone he wanted to be with, and he was going to hold on tight for as long as she'd let him. *Forever* he hoped. Her name whispered through his mind as he opened the garage and started his old Chevy. The truck had seen better days, but at least it had an intact windshield. One small layer of protection if bullets flew again.

He frowned, pulling out his cell phone and hitting Redial. Skylar needed to stay put until he got there. Stay safe. He left a message when she didn't pick up. Told her to do them both a favor and cooperate for a change.

As much as he was ready for a second chance at the job he'd once loved, he was ready for a second chance at building his dreams. A wife. Children. A happy, chaotic home.

All the things he'd been so close to having a lifetime ago.

The thought was as bittersweet as the last snowfall in the mountains.

The end of winter beauty.

The beginning of spring growth.

The way it should be.

The way Gabriella would have wanted it.

But his eyes misted anyway.

Because, saying goodbye to the past wasn't easy.

No matter how many times it had been said before.

And no matter how wonderful saying hello to the future would be.

EIGHTEEN

There wasn't one face that Skylar recognized.

She combed over the twelve photos the sheriff handed her, frustrated by her failure.

She'd seen the perp, had carved his face deep into her memories so that she wouldn't forget.

"He's not here."

"You're sure?"

"The guy I saw had white-blond hair and a thin face. None of these guys have both those things."

"Could be he has bleached hair. Lots of people are doing that, nowadays."

"Bleached hair, brown hair, it doesn't matter. I know the face I saw, and it's not in this pile."

"I'll have Sampson come in tomorrow. Maybe he can pick the guy out."

"Not if he saw what I saw, and I'm pretty confident he did," she muttered, grabbing her purse from the floor.

"Too bad. These were my top twelve candidates for the crime. Half of them are New Day members."

"Are any of them a Clovis?"

"One. He's the one I thought you'd ID." The sheriff shrugged.

"Maybe if you let me see the other brother's photo, we'd have a match."

"The younger brother was only brought in for questioning. Never arrested, so I've got no mug shot."

That didn't sound right.

Didn't sound like what Jonas's father had discovered.

"Too bad, because I know I'd recognize the guy if I saw him again."

"Then, how about we take a ride out to the compound? See if we can spot him?"

An odd suggestion.

At least, in Skylar's mind it was.

During her days on the force, she had done things by the book, and that hadn't included taking a potential witness into the enemy's lair.

Maybe things were different in small towns, but the thought of driving out to the compound with the sheriff made her skin crawl.

She couldn't put her finger on why.

Didn't bother trying.

She'd had the same unsettled feeling moments before she'd been gunned down by a supposed friend. No matter the reason for it, she wouldn't ignore the warning it conveyed.

"Thanks for the offer, but I'll wait until tomorrow. It'll save you a trip if Jonas and I go together."

"Whatever is easiest for you. Of course, I don't mind making two trips out there. I need to ask a few questions anyway." He smiled, but something hard and ugly flashed in his eyes, and Skylar backed toward the door.

"Like I said, I'll go when Jonas can."

"You two are an item?"

"We're…friends." More than that, but it wasn't the sheriff's business, and she didn't know his reasons for asking.

"Just pals, then?"

"That's right."

"So, he won't miss you all that much when you head back to New York? Won't get on a plane and rush off to find you?"

More odd questions, and Skylar's unease grew.

"Who knows? Listen, I really need to go. Thanks for letting me look at the mug shots. I'm sorry I couldn't be more helpful." She opened the door, breathed a sigh of relief when she stepped into the corridor.

Overreacting.

She had to be.

He was the sheriff. By most accounts, a good one. She had no reason to doubt his motives. No reason to suspect him of anything.

No reason except that *feeling*.

That nagging, relentless, horrifying feeling that told her bullets were about to fly and that she was going to be on the receiving end of them.

She shuddered, nearly jumping out of her skin when Sheriff Smithson dropped a hand on her arm. "I'll walk you out."

"That's not necessary, Sheriff."

"I insist."

Her heart beat double-time as the sheriff led her into the lobby. Chief Deputy Mitchell was there, and he waved, offering a smile.

"Any luck with the ID?" he asked and the sheriff shook his head.

"Not this time, but we're getting close." Smithson sounded jovial and friendly, but his grip was tighter than necessary, his fingers biting through layers of cloth and pinching Skylar's skin.

"Thank you again for your time, Sheriff. I'll see you tomorrow." She broke into the conversation, pulling her arm away, walking outside into cold, crisp air, taking a deep breath to still the nervous tremors in her belly. The sheriff didn't follow her.

Had it all been her imagination?

The feeling.

The look in the sheriff's eyes.

Or was something there that needed further investigation?

No New Day member had ever been convicted of a crime in Cave Creek. Had there been convictions in Phoenix or the surrounding areas? That would be interesting to know, because if Cave Creek *was* the only town where New Day members consistently went free, that would say something about its law enforcement officers. It would say something about the sheriff.

And what it said wouldn't be good.

She got into Richard's oversize Cadillac, eager to return to the apartment and share what she'd learned with Jonas. Eager to pick his brains, find out what he thought about the sheriff's odd questions.

He was the partner she hadn't wanted.

And he'd grown on her like dandelions on a newly cut lawn. Quickly. Unexpectedly.

The thought made her smile, but it did nothing to quell her feeling of impending danger. Her hands tightened on the steering wheel, her gaze so focused on the empty road that the rattling sound and the serpentine hiss almost didn't register.

When they did she froze, her hands fisted so tightly on the steering wheel that she thought she might break it.

Something was in the car with her.

Something that hissed.

And rattled.

Something she couldn't see, but that could see her, or sense her, or whatever it was poisonous serpentine missiles did right before they struck.

Death by snake bite wasn't on her top-one-hundred list of ways she'd like to die.

She eased the car to the side of the road, slowly, slowly, *slowly* pressing down on the brake and letting her foot rest there. Letting the car idle. Afraid to move. Afraid to breathe.

Rattle.

Hiss.

Slither.

It was under her seat.

Right.

Under.

Her.

Seat.

Move!

Don't move!

The thoughts shouted through her mind, but neither sounded better than the other, and both seemed like terrible ideas.

Stay in the car with a rattler and get bitten?

Try to get out of the car and get bitten?

She'd faced down gang members and hopped-up junkies with guns. She'd faced down bullets and betrayal. She'd even faced down the Sonoran Desert, but she had never faced down a snake in an enclosed space.

Ever.

And she'd never wanted to. It was bad enough seeing rattlers out in the wild, but at least there she could give them a wide berth. Here, there was nowhere to go. She and the snake were face to face. Or face to foot.

High-heeled foot.

Why had she let vanity get the better of her?

Why-oh-why-oh-why had she worn the black pumps instead of her scuffed boots to church?

Think, woman! You've got to get out of the car. Figure out a way to do it!

Hiss.

Rattle.

Was the snake moving?

Had it just bumped her foot? Was that it, sliding over her shoe?

Her heart thrummed frantically, as fast as a rabbit's.

A perfect meal for a hungry rattler.

I am not a rabbit. I am not a rabbit.

Hiss.

Slither.

She jerked her feet up, her knees banging into the dash as she scrambled for the door handle, poured herself out onto the pavement and slammed the door. Threw her back against it, breath heaving.

And realized her mistake.

The snake in the car wasn't the only one she should have been worried about. Another stood a few feet away. No fangs or rattles, no hissed warning, but she knew what she was seeing. She knew death when she was facing it down, even when it came in human form.

"Everything okay, ma'am?" The voice was smooth and deep, nothing serpentine about it, but the eyes? Even darkness couldn't hide their lifeless stare.

"If you can manage to pull a rattler out of my car, sure." She kept her voice even, tried to pretend she didn't recognize the white-blond hair and gaunt features. Tried to slide her hand into the pocket of her slacks and reach for her cell phone. Slowly. Slowly. The same way she'd stepped on the brake. Maybe if she moved slowly enough, she could stop this.

"Happens sometimes out in these parts. Especially this time of year. The weather is just warming up enough for rattlers to be out and about, but the temperature drops in the late afternoon, and they search for a warm place to sleep." He took a step closer.

Hiss. Slither. Rattle.

"Don't mind me. I'll just wait a few feet away while you look. I hate snakes." Especially human ones. She touched the key pad of her phone, tried to press 9-1-1 by feel. Hit Talk.

"I'm afraid I can't let you do that." He grabbed her wrist, the strike lightning fast, the blow knocking her hand out of her pocket and the phone to the ground.

"A phone, huh? Now, that wasn't very nice, was it? My father said you were wily. I guess he was right." He tossed the cell onto the roof of the car and dragged her toward his vehicle.

My father?

She didn't have time to think on it. Had to act. No way could she get in the car with a murderer. She slammed her heel into his instep, suddenly glad for her vanity.

He howled, backhanding her so hard she fell, stars dancing in front of her eyes.

Get up, Skylar. You stay too long in one place and you'll die there.

Tessa's voice. Her own. Jonas's. All of them shouting for her to go.

She stumbled to her feet, elbowed her attacker as he wrapped strong arms around her waist, dragging her to his car. She shoved backward, using her weight and his momentum to slam him into the door.

He shouted an obscenity, punching her in the side of the head.

Darkness.

She fought it, refusing it as she had when she'd been lying with three bullet holes in her body, blood pooling beneath her. Fought it because darkness meant death, and she wasn't going to die. Fought it because she'd come to Arizona looking for Redmond, and she'd found something better.

Some*one* better.

She shoved her arms under her attacker's, forcing his grip to loosen. Tried to run, but he grabbed a handful of her hair, yanking her back, pulling open the passenger-side door of his car. "Get in!"

Hiss!

He shoved her so hard she tumbled face-first into the seat. Her head hit the console, darkness rising up again.

Rattle!

Legs being shoved into place.

Blackness edging closer.

Reality slipping away.

The coiled serpent rearing back.

The door slamming, closing her in.

Strike!

NINETEEN

"Sit up. I can't drive with you in my seat."

Hard hands shoved Skylar upright, the movement, the pain forcing her from inky blackness.

She groaned, wiping blood from her mouth, trying to focus.

A car.

A man.

No. Not a man. The blond snake whose father had talked about Skylar.

His father.

Who? If she could figure that out, she might gain an advantage. In her situation, an advantage was imperative to survival.

And she *was* going to survive.

Please, God, let me survive.

She couldn't give the blond and his father the satisfaction of burying her body in a shallow grave somewhere.

Or a not-so-shallow one, like Redmond's.

Or no grave at all, like Stanley's.

She couldn't leave Jonas wondering what had happened, wondering if he could have saved her.

Couldn't leave Jonas.

Couldn't.

Stop!

Thoughts of cement slabs and brutal deaths and Jonas weren't going to save her. Panic wouldn't help her.

She needed to think. Needed to focus.

"Where are you taking me?"

"I guess it doesn't matter if I tell you. We're going to the compound." He turned dead eyes to her, and Skylar shuddered.

She'd seen eyes like those before in the faces of drug addicts and sociopaths. Empty eyes. Snake eyes. Killer eyes.

He'd as much as admitted it. It didn't matter if she knew where they were going, because he didn't intend to give her the opportunity to tell anyone else.

Keep your cool. Find a way out.

"You mean the New Day compound?"

"That's right. I have a couple friends that want to talk to you."

"About?"

"All the trouble you've caused."

"All I did was come to town looking for Daniel Redmond. If that caused anyone trouble, I'm sorry."

"Too late. Daniel was a no good, greedy son of a gun, and he deserved what he got. If he hadn't tried to get more than what we had agreed to, he'd still be alive. And so would you."

"I'm not dead, yet."

"You're dead. You just haven't realized it." There was no emotion in his voice, and Skylar shivered.

"He was helping you collect antiquities and sell them on the black market, wasn't he?"

"You've been digging for more than Redmond."

"I'm not the only one. The sheriff—"

He snorted, cutting off her words.

Rodger Smithson?

His father.

"You're Smithson's son, aren't you?"

"That's 'sheriff' to you. *And* to me. The old man has never been fond of being called anything else, seeing as how the job is everything to him, and he'll do anything to protect it."

"Even cover for you?"

"You think that's all he's doing? Then you're not as smart as he said."

"I think he's been using his position to make sure members of your organization stay out of jail. I think he has a vested interest in what you're doing—"

"World take over, baby! Starting with these good old United States, and ending when we own it all. Every last stretch of sand on every last beach. Every mountaintop retreat. *Everything*." The manic words spewed out, spittle flying onto the dashboard.

Crazy.

The word hovered on the tip of Skylar's tongue.

Don't say it.

Do not tell the man he's nuts.

"It takes an awful lot of money and power to overthrow the world."

"We won't lack power when the new messiah comes."

"You're stealing artifacts to finance His coming?"

"To finance dear old Dad's campaign. As long as he's sheriff, we can run things the way we want. Someone else comes nosing around, things might not be so easy for us."

"So you hired Redmond to help, and he got greedy so you killed him. What about Josiah Stanley?"

"He got soft. Didn't like the idea of killing a woman. He missed you purposely, you know that? Had you in his sights and changed his mind about taking the money we were going to pay him. You were that close to death." He held his thumb and index finger so close they were nearly touching. "Told me that himself before he walked off and left the group.

Kinda funny when you think about it. He wouldn't kill you, but you sure as shootin' didn't mind pulling the trigger on him. After all, it was you who came digging around. You who wouldn't leave well enough alone. Got all Dad's deputies and half the town fired up about knowing what happened to Redmond. No one cared before. No one would have cared ever if you hadn't showed up. You should have died out in the desert. The Redmond thing would have died with you."

"Sorry to inconvenience you."

"I don't like smart mouths." Dead eyes. Dead tone. A horror-movie villain in the flesh. She swallowed down the fear that threatened to freeze her tongue.

Keep him talking. Keep him engaged. Buy yourself more time.

"I don't like people who try to kill me."

"If I'd tried to kill you, you'd be dead. I didn't care about your investigation, didn't care if you found Redmond's body. The old man, he's a different story. He has a lot at stake, and he doesn't want to lose one bit of it. Couldn't cover up a murder, that's what he said. Not like he'd covered up other things. He talked to the Clovis boys, came up with a plan to take you into the desert and make it look like you got lost and died there. Didn't work out so well, though. Can't say I'm sorry. I've been looking forward to meeting you. Anyone who gets the old man in a tizzy is worth getting to know." He met her gaze again and grinned, his dead eyes flicking with wild life before they went cold again.

"We could stop for some coffee. Maybe get something to eat. I'd like to hear about New Day." She tried a different tactic, her eyes jumping to the side mirror.

The road wasn't usually busy at this time of evening, but there hadn't been another vehicle on it since they'd left her borrowed car. Her heart leaped with the knowledge.

Jonas.

Had he found her abandoned vehicle. Had he informed the police?

Please, God, let it be true.

"We'll get to know each other plenty when we get to the compound, but it won't be over coffee. Now shut up. Something doesn't feel right, and your chattering is distracting me from figuring out what it is."

Exactly what she wanted.

Especially with the silent road shouting its warning.

A blockade had been set up. Rescue would follow. She just had to stay alive long enough for it to reach her.

"When the new messiah—"

"I. Said. Shut. Up." A gun barrel pressed to her temple, and she froze like she had when the rattler had slithered beneath her seat.

Silence.

But she could almost hear the serpent's quiet rustling.

Darkness.

But she was sure eyes were watching.

Tension built, wave upon wave, and sweat trickled from her temple, her body stiff with fear and with the need to stay alive.

"Too quiet," the gunman muttered, lowering his weapon, stepping on the gas.

The car jerked forward. Lights pierced the darkness behind them. Not a cop car. A truck. Speeding after them, and she knew it was Jonas. Wanted to shout for him to go back as much as she wanted to scream for him to hurry.

Lights on the other side of the median, bouncing toward them. Blue and white. One, two, three cruisers.

Everything blurring as the car picked up speed.

Do you have your seat belt on? Jonas's voice in her ear, and her hands reaching, snapping the belt into place. Touching the arrowhead he'd given her. Praying, praying, praying that she'd see him again.

And then they were flying, spinning.

Gold and green and white and blue, everything bleeding together. Pain and darkness. Light and a sudden silence that filled Skylar's ears, filled her lungs until she thought she'd drown in it.

Move!

The warning screamed through her mind, and she grabbed the door handle, her fingers clumsy, her hands shaking. Smoke billowed from the hood of the car, the acrid scent of gasoline burning her nose, gagging her.

No air.

Just heat.

Scorching heat.

"Dear God, please. Help me!" She clawed at the door handle, her fingernails breaking.

The door flew open. Hard arms pulled her out. Lifted her up. Jonas. Running, his heart thudding under her ears.

And the night exploded.

Flying again.

Silence again. Pain.

Something heavy stealing her breath.

She moaned, shoving at the weight.

"Shhhhh. You're okay." Jonas's words carried through the haze of pain and confusion, and Skylar opened her eyes, looked into his face. His cheek was bleeding again, black hair falling over his forehead, straight and silky, his face chiseled and strong.

He looked like he had the night they'd met—like an ancient warrior come to life.

Her ancient warrior, and the stupid tears that always came when she was weakest, poured out.

"Don't cry, Grady."

"I'm not."

"Then, what are these?" He brushed away moisture, his hand lingering.

"My eyes are watering, because you're crushing the life out of me."

"That's the Grady I've come to love." He smiled, shifted.

"Love?"

"Why not?" He ran his hands up her arms and legs. "Anything hurt?"

"Only my pride for allowing myself to be lured out of my car." And about a million bumps and bruises and maybe a broken leg.

But her heart?

Her heart felt just fine.

"We found the snake. Animal control is getting it out. The way they tell it, the thing is a six foot—"

"I don't want to know the details. The thing slithered over my foot. Which reminds me, the next time I choose heels over boots, tell me not to." She levered up on her elbows.

Fire shot into the sky from crushed metal, etching the scene in startling clarity.

"Did Smithson get out?"

"The sheriff—"

"The sheriff is here?" She struggled to her feet, brushing away Jonas's hands.

"He helped set up the blockade, and he pulled the perp out of the car. It didn't look like the guy made it."

"The perp is his son. All this," she said waving frantically, "the sheriff is responsible. We need to find him. Stop him."

"You two okay?" Chief Deputy Mitchell ran toward them.

"Come on. We need to tell him what you know." Jonas grabbed her hand, pulled her forward, but the sheriff appeared, stepping past the burning rubble, gun drawn.

There was no time for anything. Just the quick thought that Jonas was the target.

Life for life?

Love for love?

Jonas shouted a warning, and the deputy turned, pulled his weapon too late.

Skylar shoved Jonas hard, felt the impact of the bullet shatter her collarbone, felt it tear through flesh and muscle and organ.

Felt it all again.

The darkness and the dying.

Only this time, it was Jonas's hands pressed against the wound, *his* eyes staring into hers, desperately trying to hold her to the world. *His* tears dripping onto her face, mixing with her tears, because, maybe, she'd been selfish.

And, maybe, the only man who'd ever filled her heart, she was going to leave empty. Maybe she was going to leave the one person who truly cared with nothing but what he'd had before they'd met.

Guilt.

Loss.

Dying shouldn't be so difficult.

But it was.

TWENTY

"How is she?" Chief Deputy Mitchell crossed the waiting room in three long strides. Eyes shadowed, deep lines carved around his mouth, he looked like he'd aged a decade in the past few hours.

Jonas felt like he'd aged double that.

His bones ached from tension and fear and too many minutes spent frozen by the weight of what had happened.

Blood dripping.

Gabriella's blood.

Skylar's.

"The surgeon is getting ready to close her up. We'll know more soon."

"I'm sorry, Jonas. You can't know how sorry I am." Mitchell dropped onto a chair, rubbed the bridge of his nose.

"Yeah. I think I can. The bullet that hit Skylar was meant for me."

Just like before.

Only this time it was meant to kill him, not destroy him, and this time there'd been no shock as blood bubbled up. He'd seen the bullet coming just as he'd felt Skylar slam into his chest.

Felt her fall.

Blood seeping.

He paced across the room, shoving the image aside.

Skylar was alive. Had been conscious but fading when they'd lifted her onto the ambulance.

Fighting hard.

Just like she always did.

And he was praying hard, like he hadn't in a long time.

He had to believe God's answer would mean Skylar's life. Had to.

"You okay?" Mitchell handed him a cup of coffee.

"Are you?"

"Smithson was my boss. I'm a police officer. It doesn't make sense that I didn't know what he was capable of. If I'd been on the ball, I would have closed him down years ago. Booked him for tampering with evidence or withholding it or whatever would get him thrown in jail for the longest amount of time. I wasn't, and two people are dead. An innocent woman is…" He shook his head, sipped coffee.

"She's going to be okay."

"So is he. The miserable excuse for a—"

"Throwing names around won't do anyone any good. Better to throw the book at him."

"Believe me, we're going after him with everything we have. The doctor is dressing the bullet wound, and then we'll drag him out of here in cuffs. We've already got him for attempted murder. We'll see what else we can find."

"Any hope for his son getting justice?"

"He got it. Gary Smithson is facing a far more permanent justice than I could enforce right now."

"Don't get bitter, Mitchell. It won't serve the community or you."

"You're right. Sorry. This is eating at me. An officer of the law serves the people. Not himself."

"Smithson had it backward."

"And upside down. Sideways." He ran a hand over his jaw,

shook his head. "Lots of dark stuff in this town, Sampson. It makes a guy wonder. We brought the Clovis brothers in an hour ago. They're trying to pin Redmond's murder on Gary Smithson."

"It's easy to blame something on a guy who's dead."

"Apparently so, because they're also claiming Gary murdered Josiah Stanley."

"You think it's true?"

"I don't know, but they're accessories one way or another. Whatever else we find, they'll be going to prison for a long time."

"Good." But Jonas wasn't interested in who'd be in jail on what charges. He wasn't interested in how many bad guys Cave Creek Sheriff's Department would throw the book at.

All he was interested in was seeing the waiting room door open and the surgeon walk in.

Please, God, let Skylar be okay.

"Listen, maybe this isn't the time or the place, but we have a slot to fill on the force. We need a guy like you to fill it."

"You're offering me the job?" Surprised, he faced Mitchell.

"I can't think of anyone else I'd want to offer it to. You have a reputation in your field that I think will carry over well into police work."

"I appreciate the offer, but I'm going to have to pass." He had another offer to accept. The same one that had been extended to him every year since he'd left the Shadow Wolves.

He was going back to the job he loved.

Whatever happened today.

But, please, let it be different than before.

"If you change your mind, let me know."

"I won't change my mind, but thanks."

"I'm going to head back to the station. We've got the state police coming in to start the internal investigation. My life is about to get really messy. You have my card, right? Call if—"

The door opened, and Jonas whirled around.

"Jonas!" His father raced toward him, Rayne and Debby hot on his heels.

"How is she?"

"Still in surgery."

"What are the doctors saying?" Rayne asked.

"Broken clavicle. Some internal bleeding. Punctured lung."

"We've been praying all the way here. For her and for you. You're both going to be okay. I know you will be." Debby's arms wrapped around him, and she hugged him tightly.

"Don't smother him, Mom. He's been through a lot. He needs some space."

"Mr. Sampson?" A young woman walked toward them. Surgical scrubs.

Careful meeting of the eye.

Sadness? Regret?

Please.

"I'm Jonas Sampson." His heart thundered in his chest.

"I'm Dr. Radcliff, the surgeon in charge of Skylar Grady's case. You're listed as next of kin."

"That's right." His family closed ranks around him, Debby's arm around his waist. Rayne crossing hers at the small of his back. His father's hand pressed to his shoulder.

His family.

And he wanted so desperately for Skylar to be part of it.

"I just finished closing her wound. There wasn't as much damage as we first thought. The lung is contused, but not punctured. We stopped one large bleeder, used a plate and screws to rebuild the shattered clavicle. She has a hairline fracture in her left fibula, but that should heal without intervention. She'll be sore for a while, but, barring any unforeseen complications, she should be fine."

Thank You, Lord.

"When can I see her?"

"I planned to hold off on visits until tomorrow, but...she's awake and asking for you. Is actually quite insistent that she see you. I don't want her agitated, and I don't want to give her a sedative. Go on up, but don't wear her out. The more rest she gets, the more quickly she'll heal. Room twenty. Second floor. I'm afraid I can only allow one visitor for tonight." She offered an apologetic smile to his family, a quick goodbye to all of them and walked away.

Jonas offered his own quick goodbye to his parents and Rayne, then jogged to the stairwell, taking the stairs two at a time.

He knocked on the half-open door, walked in.

Saw her covered to her chin in blankets and bandages. Swollen lip. Swollen cheek. Pale, bruised skin.

"Sky?" He touched her temple, the only place on her that didn't seem bruised or bandaged or hurting.

"Go away." But she reached blindly for his hand, held tightly.

"Is that any way to talk to the man who pulled you from a burning car?"

"It is when he wakes me up." She offered a wan smile, opened her eyes.

"Were you really sleeping?"

"Pretending to be so that the nurses would stop coming in to take my temperature."

"How many times have they been in?"

"Once, but I get irritable when I've been shot."

"Only you would have reason to know something like that, Grady." He chuckled, the sound hot and raw with everything he felt.

Relief.

Concern.

Love.

"Yeah, well, I'd prefer not to test the knowledge again."

"I'd prefer you not, either. My life is way too boring without you in it." He pulled over a chair and sat, his legs shaky from relief. Weak from it.

"I was thinking something when I was lying on the ground with that bullet in me," she said, her voice raspy and frail. "I was thinking that maybe what I'd done was selfish. Just like you said when I untied the rope on the mesa. I was thinking that if I died, you'd be right back where you were before we met. I didn't want to die before I made sure that you were going to be okay." Tears slipped down her cheeks, each one shattering a piece of Jonas's heart.

"Only you would worry about the living when you thought you were dying." He kissed her bruised knuckles, her swollen fingers. "And, for the record, no matter what happened, I wouldn't have been the same man you met in the desert. You changed me, Skylar. Made me realize I was clinging to the past more than I was moving toward the future."

"I'm glad." Her eyes drifted closed, her grip easing. "And, for the record, you've changed me, too."

Her hand went limp, her breathing heavy.

Giving in finally.

Bruised, battered, alive.

He brushed hair from her forehead, pressed his lips close to her ear, whispered. "Here's another thing for the records, if you ever jump in front a bullet meant for me again, I'll bring you out in the desert and leave you exactly where I found you."

To his surprise, she laughed, the sound ending on a soft groan. "It isn't nice to make a woman with a busted collarbone laugh."

"You're supposed to be sleeping."

"It's hard to sleep when every bone in my body hurts."

"I can call the nurse." He reached for the button, but she touched his hand.

"I have a better idea."

"What's that?"

"Tell me about you."

"You already know about me."

"Not the stuff we've already talked about. Tell me about climbing mesas and exploring the desert. Tell me what it's like to feel like you belong where most people wouldn't dare go."

"Sky—"

"Tell me, because some day I want to go back with you. I want to walk the desert and see it through your eyes instead of the eyes of fear. I want to climb the mesa and camp in the cave, look out at the stars. Just be. With you. And God. The whole world…" Her voice faded.

Asleep?

Awake?

"Tell me. Give me something to dream about," she whispered, and he couldn't resist her.

He lifted her hand. Gently. Gently. Stroked her knuckles.

Spoke the poetry of the desert into her ear. Spoke it as he had never spoken it to another person. Sharing his heart in a way he'd never imagined he could, the words flowing with his love for Skylar.

Just as they should.

Just as he wanted them to.

God's plan, God's will, playing out through grief and joy and everything in between, bringing Jonas to exactly the place he was always meant to be.

EPILOGUE

"You didn't tell me it was going to be this hot in May." Skylar took a long swallow of lukewarm water and eyed her husband as he rolled up a sleeping bag and hooked it to his backpack. His long-sleeved shirt was unbuttoned, his chest chiseled and hard, his abdomen smooth.

He looked good.

No.

He looked great.

Too bad it was their last morning in the desert.

She was really enjoying the scenery.

She smiled, fingering the arrowhead at her neck.

A reminder of another time.

Another trip to the desert.

A reminder of how far she and Jonas had come together.

How far they still had left go.

A lifetime, stretching out in front of them. All those dreams she'd given up on, finally being fulfilled.

"I would have, but I didn't want to spoil the surprise."

"If that's your idea of a surprise, I think I'll pass next time."

"Really?" He nuzzled her neck.

"No."

"That's what I thought. I love you, Skylar. Even if you do wilt in the heat."

"Plants wilt. I'm frying."

He chuckled.

"The sun is barely up. Look." He turned her, his chest pressed to her back, his breath ruffling her hair as he pointed to the horizon.

Gold sun.

Deep pink clouds.

Blue, blue sky.

"It's just like you said it would be, Jonas. Breathtaking."

"More so when I have you to share it with."

"I almost wish we didn't have to go back." She twisted in his arms, the secret she'd been carrying for a week, begging to be told.

Would he be happy?

Sad?

Both?

"We don't. The Clovis brothers have been convicted of first degree murder. Smithson's trial won't start for another two weeks. We can stay here until it starts. Just show up when it's time to testify."

"You're forgetting a few very important things."

"Am I?"

"We're expected in New Mexico in two weeks so you can start your new job. We have a house to pack up. I have two very pressing cases that I need to tie up before then. Not to mention our anniversary."

"What anniversary?"

"Rat." She slapped his chest, and he grinned.

"One entire year married to you. I don't think I need a reminder of that. As a matter of fact, since we're going to be busy packing to move on our official anniversary, I brought your gift with me." He knelt by his pack, pulled out a small box.

"What is it?"

"Open it and see."

She lifted the lid, her eyes welling when she saw the arrowhead necklace.

"I know you have the one my grandfather made, but I wanted to give you something from my own hands."

"It's beautiful."

"*You're* beautiful." He lifted the necklace from the box, slipped it around her neck.

She held the arrowhead in her palm, squinted at the tiny letters engraved in it. "You wrote something on it?"

"It *is* our anniversary. It had to be special."

She read the words, her eyes welling again. *For the record, I love you always.*

"You're not crying, are you?"

"No."

"Really?" He traced one tear down her cheek.

"Okay. I'm crying a little. I brought your gift, too, Jonas."

"Yeah?"

"It's here." She took his hand, pressed his palm to her still-flat abdomen, saw the wonder fill his eyes.

"Are you happy?" she whispered, and he pressed his forehead to hers, looked into her eyes.

"How could I not be?"

"The memories—"

"Will always be there. The past will always be there. But this is now. This is you. Our baby. Our future." He kissed her deeply, tenderly, endlessly.

And she wanted to stay right where she was. Forever.

Wind howled. Chopper blades churned.

Reality intruded, and Jonas broke away, breathing deeply,

his eyes blazing with love and passion. "I guess that's our cue to get out of here."

"We could ignore it." She kissed him again, and he smiled.

"We could, but we have a house to set up in New Mexico. A nursery to set up, so I think it's time we got on that chopper and got on with our future." He patted her belly, and her heart swelled with love for him.

For the child they'd created.

For all that God had done.

All that He had yet to do.

Swelled because it was so filled up, it could do nothing else.

"You know what, Jonas Sampson? I think you're right," she said.

And Jonas swept her into his arms and carried her toward the chopper and all the beauty and trials and joy God had in store for them.

* * * * *

Dear Reader,

Tragedy often brings us to a place of choices. Will we hold tight to our faith or will we doubt what we believe? Jonas Sampson has stood in that place. After the murder of his wife and unborn son, he questions his purpose and struggles to hold his faith. When he's asked to help find missing private investigator Skylar Grady, he agrees. But getting Skylar back to safety is more complicated than he expects. As he and Skylar work to uncover a killer's plan, Jonas must search his heart and learn that no matter how far we roam, God is only a prayer away.

I hope you enjoyed reading *Lone Defender* as much as I enjoyed writing it! I love to hear from readers. If you have time, drop me a line at shirlee@shirleemccoy.com.

Wherever you go, whatever you do, may you feel the fullness of God's ever-present love.

Blessings,

Shirlee McCoy

Questions for Discussion

1. Skylar Grady is a survivor. What characteristics do you think make a person a survivor?

2. How has Skylar's past shaped her personality and character?

3. Jonas has suffered a horrible tragedy. What is his response to it?

4. How strong is his faith before the tragedy?

5. Does that change after the murder of his wife and son?

6. Is it hard to keep believing in the goodness of God's plan when your life seems to be falling apart?

7. What promises has God made regarding difficulties in life?

8. Are there Bible verses you find comfort in during troubling times? What are they?

9. Jonas's guilt leads him to give up his work as a border patrol agent. Do you think that was the right decision?

10. Have you ever made a decision based on emotion and regretted it?

11. What is it that draws Jonas and Skylar together? Would you characterize them as similar or different in personality?

12. Skylar has a difficult time trusting others, but she does trust Jonas. Why?

13. Jonas knows that he must move on with his life, but doing so isn't easy. What is it that leads him to finally move forward?

14. Is there something in your past that keeps you from moving forward into God's plan for your life?

15. What Biblical principles guide us in dealing with past trauma and heartache?

INSPIRATIONAL

Inspirational romances to warm your heart & soul.

Love Inspired®
SUSPENSE

TITLES AVAILABLE NEXT MONTH

Available October 11, 2011

NIGHTWATCH
The Defenders
Valerie Hansen

THE CAPTAIN'S MISSION
Military Investigations
Debby Giusti

PRINCESS IN PERIL
Reclaiming the Crown
Rachelle McCalla

FREEZING POINT
Elizabeth Goddard

LISCNM0911

REQUEST YOUR FREE BOOKS!
2 FREE RIVETING INSPIRATIONAL NOVELS
PLUS 2 FREE MYSTERY GIFTS

Love Inspired®
SUSPENSE

YES! Please send me 2 FREE Love Inspired® Suspense novels and my 2 FREE mystery gifts (gifts are worth about $10). After receiving them, if I don't wish to receive any more books, I can return the shipping statement marked "cancel". If I don't cancel, I will receive 4 brand-new novels every month and be billed just $4.49 per book in the U.S. or $4.99 per book in Canada. That's a saving of at least 22% off the cover price. It's quite a bargain! Shipping and handling is just 50¢ per book in the U.S. and 75¢ per book in Canada.* I understand that accepting the 2 free books and gifts places me under no obligation to buy anything. I can always return a shipment and cancel at any time. Even if I never buy another book, the two free books and gifts are mine to keep forever.

123/323 IDN FEHR

Name _____ (PLEASE PRINT) _____

Address _____ Apt. #

City _____ State/Prov. _____ Zip/Postal Code

Signature (if under 18, a parent or guardian must sign)

Mail to the **Reader Service:**
IN U.S.A.: P.O. Box 1867, Buffalo, NY 14240-1867
IN CANADA: P.O. Box 609, Fort Erie, Ontario L2A 5X3

Not valid for current subscribers to Love Inspired Suspense books.

**Are you a subscriber to Love Inspired Suspense
and want to receive the larger-print edition?
Call 1-800-873-8635 or visit www.ReaderService.com.**

* Terms and prices subject to change without notice. Prices do not include applicable taxes. Sales tax applicable in N.Y. Canadian residents will be charged applicable taxes. Offer not valid in Quebec. This offer is limited to one order per household. All orders subject to credit approval. Credit or debit balances in a customer's account(s) may be offset by any other outstanding balance owed by or to the customer. Please allow 4 to 6 weeks for delivery. Offer available while quantities last.

Your Privacy—The Reader Service is committed to protecting your privacy. Our Privacy Policy is available online at www.ReaderService.com or upon request from the Reader Service.

We make a portion of our mailing list available to reputable third parties that offer products we believe may interest you. If you prefer that we not exchange your name with third parties, or if you wish to clarify or modify your communication preferences, please visit us at www.ReaderService.com/consumerschoice or write to us at Reader Service Preference Service, P.O. Box 9062, Buffalo, NY 14269. Include your complete name and address.

LISUS11B

Sophie Bartholomew loves all things Christmas.
Caring for an orphaned little boy
makes this season even more special.
And so does helping a scarred cop move past his pain
and see the bright future that lies ahead...

Since the moment Kade had appeared at Ida June's wreath-laden door behind a spotless, eager Davey, Sophie had had butterflies in her stomach. A few hours ago, they'd been having pizza and getting better acquainted, but she felt as though she'd known him much longer than a few jam-packed days. In reality, she didn't know him at all, but there was something, some indefinable pull between them.

Maybe their mutual love for a little lost boy had connected their hearts.

"Christmas is about a child," she said. "Maybe God sent him."

One corner of Kade's mouth twisted. "Now you sound like my great-aunt."

"She's a very smart lady."

"More than I realized," he said softly, a hint of humor and mystery in the words. "A good woman is worth more than rubies."

"What?" Sophie tilted her head, puzzled. Though she recognized the proverb, she wasn't quite sure where it fit into the conversation.

"Something Ida June said."

"Ida June and her proverbs." Sophie smiled up at him. "What brought that one on?"

Kade was quiet for a moment, his gaze steady on hers. He gently brushed a strand of hair from the shoulder of her sweater, an innocent gesture that, like a cupid's arrow, went straight to her heart.

"You," he said at last.

Sophie's heart stuttered. Though she didn't quite get what he meant or why he was looking at her so strangely, a mood, strong and fascinating, shimmered in the air.

Their eyes held, both of them seeking for answers neither of them had. All Sophie had were questions she couldn't ask. So far, every time she'd approached the topic of his life in Chicago, Kade had closed himself in and locked her out.

A woman above rubies, he'd said. Had he meant her?

Sophie senses Kade's eagerness to connect. But can she convince him to open his heart to love—and to God? Don't miss THE CHRISTMAS CHILD by Rita® Award-winning author, Linda Goodnight, on sale October 2011 wherever Love Inspired books are sold!

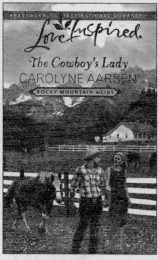

Love Inspired® SUSPENSE

RIVETING INSPIRATIONAL ROMANCE

Fire captain Mitch Andrews can't forget the three young children he saved from a suspicious fire—one that left them orphans. He knows foster mother Jill Kirkpatrick will love them. But when the kids and Jill are put in terrible danger, Mitch is willing to risk everything to keep a family of five together.

NIGHTWATCH

by VALERIE HANSEN

THE DEFENDERS

Available October 2011 wherever books are sold.

www.LoveInspiredBooks.com

LIS44460